CW00495883

New Ghost Stories II

The Fiction Desk Anthology Series
Volume Eight

Edited by Rob Redman

The Fiction Desk

First published in 2014 by The Fiction Desk Ltd.

This collection © The Fiction Desk Ltd.
Individual stories © their respective authors.

This book is sold subject to the condition that it shall not, by the way of trade or otherwise, be lent, resold, hired out, or otherwise circulated without the publisher's prior consent in any form of binding or cover other than that in which it is published and without a similar condition, including this condition, being imposed on the subsequent purchaser.

ISBN 978-0-9927547-4-7

The Fiction Desk
PO Box 116
Rye
TN31 9DY

Please note that we do not accept postal submissions.
See our website for submissions information.

www.thefictiondesk.com

The Fiction Desk Ltd
Registered in the UK, no 07410083
Registered office: 3rd Floor, 207 Regent Street, London, W1B 3HH

Printed and bound in the UK by Imprint Digital.

Contents

Introduction 7
Rob Redman

Incomers 9
Amanda Mason

The Bear Got Me 29
Matthew Licht

Next to Godliness 45
Matt Plass

The Table 57
Tamsin Hopkins

The Armies 69
Miha Mazzini

The Time of Your Life 81
Lucinda Bromfield

End of the Rope 89
Melanie Whipman

Hell for Leather 99
Bernie Deehan

Twice a Day with Water 109
Die Booth

Watching Kate & Gustav 117
Alice Adams

In Yon Green Hill to Dwell 125
Jane Alexander

Tam Lin 137
Traditional

About the Contributors 145

Introduction

Rob Redman

What, has this thing appeared again tonight?

We didn't really intend to publish a second volume of ghost stories; but then, we didn't really intend to publish the first one either. It's not always up to us. We have to do what the stories tell us.

There's always a little supernatural fiction in our anthologies, but last year we found ourselves with so much good material that we had to publish a special anthology dedicated to it. Featuring stories from Matthew Licht, Joanne Rush, Amanda Mason, Jason Atkinson, and many more, the first *New Ghost Stories* turned out to be one of our strongest anthologies to date.

This year, it's happened again: a host of fine ghost stories waiting in the wings. And so here we are, a dreaded sight twice seen, moving silently through the gloom of the unlit stage, all ready to harrow you with fear and wonder.

As usual, you'll have seen some of us before: Matt Plass, Miha Mazzini, Die Booth, Matthew Licht, and Amanda Mason have all trod these boards on other nights.

But if familiar faces are the most comforting when it's dark, don't be shy of the newcomers: Tamsin Hopkins, Lucinda Bromfield, Melanie Whipman, Bernie Deehan, Alice Adams, and Jane Alexander are all worth watching.

Jane Alexander's story won the 2014 Fiction Desk ghost story competition, and draws on the traditional Scottish ballad *Tam Lin*. You don't need to know that poem to appreciate Jane's story, but if you're curious, it's reprinted in full at the end of the book.

'Incomers' is Amanda's second ghost story for The Fiction Desk, following 'No Good Deed' in New Ghost Stories. *It's good to have her back, but not all returns are so welcome...*

Incomers

Amanda Mason

The ceiling is low. It sags a little, and its exposed beams are scarred and pockmarked. The house looked bigger online; there was the impression of luxury, of space. But the front door opens straight into a tiny living room crammed with tastefully mismatched furniture. Framed watercolour prints crowd the walls, and a crocheted blanket is folded carefully over the back of the sofa. Jetsam Cottage.

Behind her, Jamie drops his bag onto the floor and hooks an arm around her waist.

'This is nice,' he says. 'Cosy.'

Emma's not disappointed. She won't be disappointed.

She leans back against him for a moment and closes her eyes.

'Okay?' he asks.

'Yes.'

The cottage is tucked away in a narrow cobbled yard and the afternoon light is already fading.

The windows rattle.

She shivers.

'Cold?'

'A bit.'

The air is damp in here, salty.

'Do you know how to light the stove?' she asks.

A modern wood burner stands in the fireplace; logs piled neatly either side of it. She wouldn't know where to start.

'Sure,' Jamie says, pulling her closer, kissing her neck, making her smile.

'Good.'

Up the narrow staircase, the whitewashed bedroom offers, as promised, a sea view, and Emma looks out across the harbour. The heavy grey waves shift underneath the darkening sky and the wind moans. This is a present from Jamie, a few days away, their first trip together.

She'd been disappointed at first, when he'd handed her the envelope instead of the small gift-wrapped box she'd been hoping for. But he'd made the card himself, using a photograph of the village, and along with a brief message – *Merry Christmas, Emma!* – he'd written the dates and details of the cottage.

Lots of love, Jamie. xxx

The bedroom is plain and simple, and it's not that bad, she decides. There's a rag rug, a brass bedstead, a wardrobe and a chest of drawers. It doesn't take long to unpack: she works quickly, trying to ignore the chill.

The bathroom across the landing is dark. A tap is dripping. Directly opposite the door an old mirror set in a heavy wooden frame hangs over the sink, and Emma considers her reflection. The image is blurry in the faint winter light; there are two women where there should be one. She pulls on the light switch; the weight on the cord is sea-worn green glass and it swings gently, tapping against the wall.

There she is all alone. The electric light is unforgiving: her nose and cheeks are red and her long dark hair is a mess. She should tidy herself up a bit.

The top left hand corner of the mirror is grubby. She reaches up and wipes it with her thumb, but it's not dirt, the glass is stained somehow, foxed. Behind her, a stair creaks. Jamie.

She turns, but the landing is empty.

The mattress sinks as she sits on the bed and she listens for a moment to the wind outside. Louder now. Closer. She runs her hand over the blue-and-white patchwork quilt. The fabric, heavy and slightly damp, catches against her fingers. She wonders briefly if the bed has been aired properly and then smiles as she thinks of Jamie, his warm heavy limbs wrapped around her, his breath on her neck, skin against skin.

But, as ever, another image intrudes; she rolls over, kicking the sheets back, blonde hair fanning out over the pillow, whispers and sighs and smiles as he leans over to kiss her – Sarah.

'Em?'

His voice drifts up from the living room.

'What?'

But his reply is lost as the wind swoops down the chimney. Emma glances out of the window one more time before going downstairs.

They eat at the small table set underneath the living room window. The stove throws out a warm orange glow and Jamie has found candles to light, or maybe he brought them along. He certainly remembered to bring some music, their music, playing softly in the background, low and familiar.

'Emma.'

She's been daydreaming; she's barely touched her food.

'Sorry?'

'You were miles away.'

'Sorry.'

'I thought we could go for a walk. Down by the harbour, maybe call in at the pub.'

'Sure.'

'Only if you want to.'

'No. That would be nice.'

She can break in her new boots.

Three nights and two days. Not much time at all, when you think about it.

She looks out of the window.

The other cottages are dark, she notices. Holiday lets and second homes, their owners are far away, somewhere brighter, somewhere warmer.

Buffeted this way and that by the wind, Emma clings to Jamie as they struggle along the quay. The cobblestones are slick under her feet, and the legs of her jeans are sodden. In the distance the windows of the pub are picked out in fairy lights that flash intermittently as a Christmas tree by the front door shudders, frantically shedding tinsel into the night. The sky is black, starless, and Emma shivers.

'Why do you do that?' he asks.

They each have a glass of red wine and are sitting by the open fire, their faces and fingers tingling.

'Do what?'

She's been gazing idly at the photos on the wall, generations of lifeboat crews arranged in front of a succession of boats. Only in the more recent pictures does anyone smile.

'Whenever we speak to anyone, your voice changes.'

'What?'

'You change your accent.'

'No I don't.'

She can hear them, the flat vowels of her childhood.

'There.'

He looks pleased. As if he's caught her out.

'Why do you do that?' he says

'I don't know.'

It's the truth. She can't help it.

He sips his wine and looks around the room and Emma feels that tug again, that overwhelming rush that thrills and terrifies her so. She can't quite believe they're here, together.

'What?' he says.

She's been caught out. Staring.

They've agreed to take things slowly, to give themselves some time.

'Nothing,' she says, blushing.

The pub is quiet. People are saving themselves for tomorrow, for New Year's Eve.

Two more days.

Jamie settles back in his seat and behind him the door opens and another couple blow in, shaking their hats and flapping their waterproof coats. The woman runs her fingers through her bright blonde hair and smiles up at her husband. He turns to the bar as she glances across the room and, too late, Emma looks away.

'Where are you staying?'

'Oh,' Emma picks up her wine and takes a sip. They've been nothing but perfectly friendly, these two strangers, but she doesn't like the feeling that she and Jamie have been taken up, taken over. By Lizzie and John.

'Jetsam Cottage,' says Jamie.

John looks puzzled for a moment, but then his expression clears.

'Ah,' he says, 'Janet Cottage. The witch house.'

'John.'

His wife is frowning.

'What? Everyone knows about poor old Janet Bone.'

'It's just a story,' Lizzie says to Emma. Underneath the table, Emma puts her hand on Jamie's leg, squeezing gently, hoping he'll take the hint.

'Here.'

John is on his feet now, and he goes to the bar, where he rifles through a heap of books wedged behind the RNLI collection box.

'Sorry,' says Lizzie, 'he's a typical incomer about ghosts and legends.'

She smiles conspiratorially at Emma who in turn feels a sharp spike of jealousy that has nothing to do with second houses or sailing boats or the ridiculous diamond on Lizzie's left hand. The two of them seem to belong together, to fit so neatly.

Sitting quietly next to Jamie, she feels awkward, out of place.

An incomer.

'Ghosts?' she says.

John has found the book he's looking for.

'Here you are,' he says, sitting down again. 'A photo of a witch, an actual genuine witch.'

He's holding the book open at a reproduction of a sepia photograph, *Fisher Girls* by Edwin Franks, taken in 1887.

A group of women are posed in front of a fishing boat on the beach. They are all young, dressed in closely fitted shirts, buttoned to the throat, and heavy skirts and aprons. They wear ruffled cotton bonnets and rough work boots, and have unfastened their shirt sleeves, rolling them up to the elbow as the only visible concession to the summer heat. Emma feels sweat prickling around her neck just looking at them.

'There.'

John points to the girl standing to the extreme left. She's holding a fishing net and gazing steadfastly out to sea. The bonnet covers her hair and obscures her face; she's just a girl, standing on a beach.

'She doesn't look like a witch,' says Jamie.

John takes back the book and flicks through the pages.

'Even so,' he says, 'she was still accused of murder, of causing death by drowning by means of witchcraft.'

'In court?' asks Emma.

'Well, no, not exactly. Her name was Janet Bone and the story is she was being courted by a local man, Isaac Vasey. But he met someone else and broke things off with her.'

'Who?' asks Emma.

'Just a girl, a girl from the village, no one special,' says John, 'So, anyway, Janet is dumped by Isaac and she starts to, well, stalk him, I suppose. She makes it her business to be standing by his boat, a coble called Good Fortune, whenever he's due to set sail. She doesn't say a word, mind. She just stands and stares at him.'

'Which is very clever of her,' says Lizzie, 'because the fishermen here won't go to sea if they meet a woman on the way to their boat. They think it's bad luck, you know?'

'I'm sorry?'

Emma can't quite follow this.

'It's a local thing,' says Lizzie. 'The men won't put out to sea if they meet a woman as they walk to their boat, very bad luck.'

'I still can't see how that would ever be practical,' says John, 'but anyway...'

They've told this story before, Emma realises. It's one of their routines.

'He has to go to sea in the end, doesn't he? He'll starve otherwise, him and the other men in the coble.'

'And their families,' says Lizzie.

'So one day, despite meeting Janet out there on the quay, they put to sea.'

'And he drowned?'

Emma can't help it; she wants them to get to the point, to get it over with. She doesn't like this story, she doesn't like the way they relish it so.

'They're hit by one of the worst storms in living memory,' says John. 'The boat is lost with all hands. The Good Fortune and three other cobles. Eleven men dead in total.'

'Plus three of the lifeboat crew,' says Lizzie, 'all of them volunteers.'

'It hardly seems fair to blame her for that,' says Jamie.

'But she was seen,' says John, 'seen in her cottage calling up a storm.'

'But who saw her? What did they see, exactly?' says Emma.

'Well, that part's a bit vague,' says John, 'but after a while word gets around the village that Janet Bone called up the storm that killed Isaac Vasey and all those other men.'

'Gossip,' says Jamie.

'Gossip that doesn't die down,' says John.

Was it her, Emma wonders, the young nameless woman who took away Isaac, only to lose him anyway. Was she the one who started the rumours?

'You have to remember that people round here were very superstitious in those days,' says Lizzie, her clear round vowels carrying across the room. 'They still are, really.'

'But they can't have arrested her, can they?' asks Emma.

Not for witchcraft, surely.

'No. No, of course not. She was... well, I suppose she was shunned, ignored. I mean, she still lived in her cottage, but her parents were dead and she lived there alone.'

Alone in that dark, damp little house.

'Then what happened?' asks Jamie.

'She drowned herself, in the end,' says John.

Not hard in those heavy skirts.

But still, hard enough.

'Poor thing,' says Emma.

'The house has been called Janet Cottage for as long as we've been here,' says Lizzie. 'I wonder why the new owners have changed it.'

'Here it is,' says John. He's found another photograph in the book. A snapshot, less carefully composed than the portrait of the girls, it shows the little cobbled yard, the sandstone cottage and the darkened windows. The name doesn't matter. It hasn't really changed at all.

Emma's had enough now. She wants to get away from John and Lizzie. She wants to have Jamie to herself for a while. She plays with her empty glass as the conversation turns to sailing and she waits for the evening to end.

She still can't sleep.

Jamie is snoring gently. Huddled under the duvet, he doesn't seem to feel the cold. She lies still for a while, listening to the wind, the incessant boom of it, lifting tiles, shifting chimney pots. It whistles around the house, slicing through the floorboards.

The windows shudder and down in the yard something, a bin probably, rattles and skids over the cobbles.

It's vicious.

When she can stand it no longer, she slips carefully out of bed and crosses the room. She pulls back one of the curtains and presses her face against the windowpane. She still can't see the storm, but she can feel it.

She's done this before. She's stood at this window looking out to sea.

Waiting.

Worrying.

Behind her, a floorboard sighs as someone steps lightly across the room.

She'll go downstairs, get something to drink.

She moves quietly, although Jamie lies still, dead to the world.

The lights in the kitchen make her flinch, so she turns them back off. The stone flags are cold under her feet. She'll get a drink and get back to bed. She finds a glass, lets the tap run for a moment or two and then fills it.

How do you call up a storm?

She licks her lips.

It's too cold to be standing here, she knows. She should get into bed with Jamie. She could snuggle up to him, wake him, let him hold her, let him warm her.

She rolls over, kicks back the sheets.

No.

Scatter the water on the dusty flagstones, sweep up the wind, send it out into the world.

She feels that tug again, followed by a sharp, pitching sense of loss, strong enough to take her breath away.

She can't help it.

Jamie, she thinks.

And then –

Sarah.

If only she can be good enough, better.

Better than Sarah who left Jamie. Who broke his heart. Who won't leave her be.

She drinks her water slowly, standing in the dark, barefoot on the shiny new linoleum.

'Hey,' he says.

Emma rolls over in bed; the sheets on his side are cold.

'Time to get up.'

He's holding a mug of tea.

'I'll make breakfast, shall I?'

She takes the tea, tries to smile, tries to speak, she clears her throat but the words won't come. God, it's early.

She can't remember getting into bed.

He kisses her quickly, too quickly.

'Come on then,' he says, placing the mug on the bedside table. 'Breakfast in five minutes.'

Emma's head aches as she tries to eat her scrambled eggs. Opposite her Jamie reads the paper and drinks his coffee. He's obviously been up for hours. He could have woken her; he could have stayed in bed with her. That's why they're here, after all. To be together. Outside, the wind has dropped and the sky has cleared.

'You okay, Em?'

She nods. Their time together, just the two of them, is ticking away and she wishes she could start the day over.

She licks her lips. Her mouth is still dry.

Jamie carries the map. Not that they really need one: they're only going for a short walk, along the coastal path to the next village. But by the time they've got to the top of the cliff, Emma's legs are burning. The way is steep and rough, and to her inexperienced eyes, the drop to the beach is alarming. She pauses for a moment, turning to look at the view. Houses curve around the bay, and beyond the pub a stubby sandstone pier provides shelter for the few boats at their moorings. It looks safe, self-contained, familiar.

'You fit?'

Jamie isn't out of breath.

'Sure.'

She wishes he'd take her hand as they walk, but he sets off briskly, leading the way. Jamie loves to walk, to hike and climb and sail, and it's one of the things she loves about him, this fearless enthusiasm. She turns her back on the view and does her best to keep up.

Lunch is fish and chips at the next village, and as they eat Jamie consults the map.

'Which way shall we go back?'

'Bus?'

It's only half a joke. After a mile, Emma's new boots had begun to chafe. After five, walking had become a red-hot agony. She's already been to the ladies' loo in the cafe to plaster over the blisters on the backs of her ankles. One has burst, exposing raw and angry flesh.

'We can go inland,' says Jamie, turning the map to show her. 'There's a path through some woodland and then we can cross the main road here and drop back into the village.'

'How far is it?'

Emma flexes her foot under the table. She's not going to complain. She's not going to whine.

Jamie doesn't answer.

'Or we could just walk back along the beach, if the tide's right.'

'Are you sure?'

Emma's heard horror stories of people being trapped by the incoming tide. Trapped and then rescued. Or maybe not.

'Yeah, we can check the tides down on the quay.'

He folds the map and starts to eat.

'How do you know that? About the tides?'

'Because I've done it before. A few years ago.'

She could ask.

She doesn't.

But the question hangs there between them all the same. Gleaming.

She picks up her fork and tries to sound bright, unconcerned.

'Okay, we'll do that then,' she says.

The day goes too quickly, in the end. Even though they take their time walking back along the beach, stopping now and then to explore rock pools or to take photographs. Once they have to stop to let Emma change the plasters on her ankles, and she has to shove the old bloodied bits of dressing into her coat pocket. By the time they make their way around the cliff into the bay, her legs are trembling; she can't remember when she last walked so far.

'Well done, you,' Jamie says, unlocking the front door. 'New boots can be a bit of a bugger.'

She tries to smile before making her way upstairs.

Emma lays back in the bath, watching the steam rise, condensation clinging to the mirror. One more night and one more day and they'll have to go back; she to her flat, Jamie to his. She doesn't want to let him go. Maybe she can persuade him to stay over with her, when they get back.

She closes her eyes. Her legs ache and her feet are sore. She wishes she'd taken more photographs. She imagines the two of them looking at them one day, *the time we stayed in that little cottage...* No. *The first time we stayed...*

She's drifting. She can feel the thud of her pulse as she slips further under the water, the heat flooding through her limbs. They'll stay in tonight, just the two of them, here in their cottage. They'll bring the wine to bed, see in the New Year together and put the old year, with all its disappointments and heartbreak behind them. Sarah won't matter anymore. She'll make him forget.

Her heart slows as she floats. Oh, God, how she loves him, how she wants him to love her. If only he could see...

If he could only see that he can't leave. She won't allow it. She'll show him what she can do.

'Emma.'

The door crashes open and Emma pulls herself upright, struggling to catch her breath.

There's a man in the doorway. A stranger.

'Emma,' he says, 'didn't you hear me?'

She's shivering. She must have fallen asleep.

'Emma? Are you okay?'

He's holding his phone.

'I... Yes. You startled me,' she says.

The water is cold.

'It's John,' he says. 'He and Lizzie are going to see the New Year in at the pub and he thought we'd like to join them.'

'Oh.'

She draws her knees up, and clutches at them, goose bumps pulling at her skin. She feels unsettled, raw.

'So? Shall we?'

No.

'Oh. Yes. If you like.'

No.

'Great.'

Jamie pulls the door closed behind him and Emma can hear him speaking to John as she gets out of the bath. She stands on unsteady legs, water dripping onto the floorboards.

The cold has seeped into her, into her bones and she has the feeling that she's in the wrong place, she has the curious sensation that her skin is not her own. She wraps herself in a towel, teeth chattering.

She'd fallen asleep. That's all.

They find a table eventually. The four of them crammed into a corner as the pub fills up, getting noisier, rowdier. In the opposite corner some people start playing folk music and gradually everyone joins in with songs Emma's never heard before, cheering and whooping and chorusing in unsteady harmony.

Behind the bar, the clock ticks slowly towards midnight.

The New Year, when it comes, finds Emma stuck between Lizzie and John as they join in with Auld Lang Syne, and Jamie's kiss, when he finally pushes his way to her, is tainted with beer and cigarette smoke. He lets go of her and turns to hug Lizzie. The noise in the pub makes Emma's head ache.

The tread on the stair wakes her.

'Jamie?'

She sits up.

'Jamie.'

He's not there.

She finds him in the kitchen.

'What time is it?'

'Early.'

He's fully dressed, eating a fried egg sandwich and drinking coffee.

'Sorry,' he says. 'I didn't mean to disturb you.'

She wraps her arms around herself. She hadn't thought to bring a dressing gown.

'What's happening?' she asks.

'I'm going out for a sail with John and Lizzie.'

'Oh. When was all this arranged?'

'Last night. I told you last night.'

Maybe he did, she can't remember. She doesn't really remember getting home.

Jamie stands.

'Well, I'll come with you, shall I?' she says.

It won't take her long to get dressed.

'No, you don't need to; it's not really your sort of thing is it? And anyway, you're still half asleep.'

He's barely paying attention to her as he puts his mug and plate in the sink.

'We won't be out for long. Why don't you go back to bed? We can all go out for lunch when we get back.'

He's picking up his coat, not even waiting for an answer.

'Promise you won't be long.'

It's all she can find to say and Jamie smiles.

'I promise,' he says.

He kisses her gently on the cheek on his way out.

It's their last day.

She's no warmer back under the duvet. Chilled to the bone, she gives up trying to go back to sleep and dresses as quickly as she can, forcing her sore feet back into her walking boots.

In the bathroom, she brushes her teeth, avoiding her reflection, fighting the sinking feeling that she's somehow failed a test; a test no one had told her about. They've had a good time, haven't they? They'll come back, won't they?

He would have taken Sarah sailing.

She glances up into the mirror. The stain she'd noticed seems bigger now, rusty clouds seem to swirl down from the top of the frame, masking her face, casting shadows.

No he wouldn't. He'd have stayed in bed with Sarah. They'd have hidden themselves under the duvet, giggling about John and Lizzie and their second home and their stupid boat.

Incomers.

People who don't fit.

Tears well up in her eyes. If she could only work out where it went wrong, where she went wrong. If only she could have yesterday back again and get it right.

She'll go downstairs and light the fire and make some lunch, have it ready for when they get back. She'll make a cup of tea first though. She feels grubby and sick, and her head aches. She licks her lips and looks more closely at her reflection and her breath fogs the mirror a little. She breathes harder and traces out a swirling pattern of spiralling waves in the mist; rising, curving, falling over and over. She rubs her fingertips over the staining on the glass.

Her breath beads on the mirror, the cloud smears under her fingers, billowing across the sea. Her heartbeat quickens.

You can sweep up a storm. Or you take your broom and scatter water with it. Spring water is good. Spring water mixed with a little salt.

It's no more than he deserves.

It's only when the water overflows, spilling over her legs and feet, staining the floorboards, that she realises she's turned on the taps, that she's flooding the little bathroom.

God, it's pathetic, standing here, crying like this.

She rubs at her tears and plunges her hands into the sink, pulling at the plug and fumbling at the taps with clumsy fingers.

Maybe she will lie down again, just for a little while.

The firework wakes her. Left over from last night, she supposes, blinking in the gloom. Jamie must have left her to sleep the day away, if he's bothered to check up on her at all.

She sits up and looks at her watch. It's not quite midday.

A gust of wind strikes the house.

Not dark.

Rain spatters against the windows.

A storm.

Her headache is worse.

Downstairs in the kitchen a tap is running.

'Jamie?'

She shuts it off and goes into the living room.

The stove is grey and cold.

Not a firework, a maroon.

The fishermen hear it, and they run down to the harbour, to the boathouse.

All those photos in the pub; the crews in their cork life jackets standing in front of the lifeboat.

By the time she gets to the quay, a small crowd has gathered. Tourists, mainly. Families with small children, people who see the launch of the lifeboat as something exciting and are willing to brave the filthy weather to watch for a while.

'What's happened?' she asks the man next to her, the wind snatching her words away.

'I think there's a yacht in trouble,' he says, lifting his camera to take one last shot.

Emma watches the lifeboat, an impossibly small inflatable, as it bounces across the harbour and then turns, heading out to sea.

They should be back now. They must be back.

She struggles to recall that first night in the pub, John and Lizzie and their house and their boat, the name of their boat. But it flutters away, just out of her grasp.

The rain falls in torrents, sharp stinging needles bouncing off the sandstone flags, pooling and eddying in the howling gale. Emma stands staring out to sea, watching the lifeboat, no more than a smudge of grey and orange now, fight its way through the waves before it vanishes beyond the headland. The wind gusts and the waves rise, smacking up against the pier before dissolving into salty clouds.

What has she done?

If she could just take it all back and start again.

Get it right.

There's nothing more to see and the crowd is starting to feel the cold and the wet; people begin to wander towards shelter.

'You should come back, pet.'

The woman's voice makes her jump.

'People don't realise, a high tide like this. You can get swept away.'

Emma nods.

'Yes,' she says.

She understands that she should go, but she doesn't move. She waits until everyone has walked back up the pier; until she's the only one left, the wind tugging at her, nudging, wrapping itself around her. She staggers a little, struggling to stay upright, unable to decide what she should do, where she should go. Trapped between the land and the sea, the sea and the sky.

She has seen this before, felt this before.

What has she done?

The clouds swirling in the mirror. Her tears.

It's no more than he deserves.

Not Sarah, after all. Never Sarah, not really.

She shouldn't have let her in, the woman in the mirror, the blurred shadow, the tread on the stair.

She's been there all along, inside the house, inside her head, nudging, whispering.

Waiting.

Janet.

Emma begins to shake, her stomach cramps.

What has she done?

She stumbles and lets go, falling to her knees as something inside her shifts and separates. No longer held within, buzzing in the back of her head, weighing her down, holding her back, a shadow steps away, out into the storm.

She understands now; too late, of course, too late.

Janet Bone.

Two women now, where there had been only one.

She can't see her, but she can feel a thickening in the air as Janet steps carefully around her.

It was no more than he deserved.

Above and around them the storm drives the tide in, the waves rising and breaking against the shore. Relentless.

On the pier, water streams from her heavy skirts as she bends over, reaching out. Her icy touch is gentle, almost kind, as Emma, soaked to the skin and seized with shuddering spasms, starts to vomit up cold clear saltwater.

Matthew Licht had a run-in with a good-sized black bear in northern Michigan. The animal ignored him utterly. Miffed, the author decided literary interspecies comeuppance was a dish best served cold. He waited nearly thirty years to pen this spine-curdling tale of ghostly paranoia. Mighty cold, up there near Barrow, well within the Arctic Circle, in the dead of winter...

The Bear Got Me

Matthew Licht

Garson Thayer didn't like driving at night, but since his internal clock, an expensive Swiss gadget, sent signals to the effect that it wasn't officially night yet, he kept going.

He was on his way to do a job for Strategic Air Command. He worked for them fairly often, couldn't help wondering why they paid stratospheric consultation fees yet refused to spring for drivers. The US Military had a near-infinite pool of uniformed serfs with valid military licenses and civilian hot rod / speedway experience. He could've used expensive travel time to review classified documents and equipment diagrams in the back seat, in a cone of light from some highly engineered inner-automobile reading apparatus.

He also wondered why SAC never sent him to Hawaii.

The answer was obvious. The missiles were aimed the other way. So he was driving to an officially uncharted location near Barrow, in the upper reaches of the USA's freezer cabinet, at three in the afternoon, according to the aforementioned internal timepiece. The dashboard clock and radio announcer expressed agreement, but the charcoal-grey outer darkness said the information was a lie. Night was coming. Night was already here. Night was outrageously cold.

The bulky extreme low-temperature Olive Drab snorkel coat, Gov't Issue, which he'd found neatly folded on the webbing seat next to his on the transport airplane, sat humped in the back seat of the car. Its coyote-fur ruff shimmered in warm breezes from the auto heater. The minimal movement caught Garson's eye in the rear-view mirror. He reached back and scrunched the parka down. Didn't want a spectral, vaguely human-shaped presence looming behind him.

He turned up the radio. Faraway civilisation sent weak music signals. 'Try to see something grand or majestic in these bleak surroundings,' he thought. 'Think where you are. Top of the world. Maybe they'll take you up in a spy plane again, to allegedly survey the Brooks Range.'

Most military outpost honchos had a decent sense of humour about squandering taxpayer dough on senseless, even ridiculous outings that sounded good on official reports, on the off-chance such reports were ever demanded or, when delivered, scrutinised. Military types had exceptionally low regard for taxpayers in general. Even though military personnel and high-end experts occasionally on the payroll had to pay taxes without fail, too.

The grey-lit spaces in the car's beaming eyesight were punctuated with grim, straight, black trees. Garson tried to picture the forest he was traversing in godly overview. Best fringe benefit of the SAC gig was streaking over topography at near-light speed in flying machines the taxpaying general public wasn't allowed to see yet. A forest on the Earth was like fur on an animal. Maybe the trees were firs. In any case, no shortage of trees, in Alaska. But the military-industrial complex would take care of the unregulated abundance soon enough. Plenty oil underground, beneath ungodly snow, ice, frost, and white.

The radio frazzed out. No use jiggling the dials. No more signal. Didn't make sense. Air base management took the trouble to disguise the vehicle as non-GI for civilian consultants to transport themselves, but couldn't, or didn't bother to, equip said vehicle with a military-spec radio.

Approximately two hundred dismal miles stretched between his current position and the cryogenic void of Barrow, which was either an Eskimo whaling port, a desolate polar bear scavenging ground, or a paradise vacation spot for penguins. Garson had never visited the place, probably wouldn't get a chance this time around. He pictured an Eskimo brothel in an off-limits igloo. Inuit croupiers at a high-stakes roulette game paid off stacks of snowflake-shaped chips while Inuit maidens in leopard seal-fur bikinis served frosty drinks in an under-the-tundra casino. Eskimo rockers in glitter parkas churned out bland covers of the Stones, Cream, Hendrix.

Arctic Circle daydreams blossomed brighter as the surrounding forest and roiling sky darkened.

Alaska's undeniable beauty involved the silence wrought by cold. Garson slowed down. Maybe the car he was driving could sustain a cruising speed of one hundred mph, but it didn't make sense to risk engine trouble in the middle of frozen nowheresville. Maybe stateside speed limits worked on the same physical principles as internal clocks.

Something moved in the rear-view mirror again. Garson thought the snorkel coat must've filled with warm air and returned to blimp-like life, reached behind to scrunch it down again, felt nothing. The coat had fallen to the car floor. He checked the mirror again and saw a dark shape in motion.

Not car-shaped. And cars move forward without any appearance of motion. The wheels roll while the body of the vehicle bobs with the occasional road contour. Animal organisms are transformed by motion. Their shapes change in obedience to a dynamic law, move or die.

The rear-view mirror took on the fascination of a movie screen. What *is* this shadowy bolus behind me? Garson slowed down further, instead of turning to look out the back window. His eyes twitched and darted to keep tabs on the road ahead.

Puffs of steam floated from a snout slightly less dark than what was around and behind it. A mouth opened to take in more air, eject more steam. Flash of indecently huge yellow fangs. A bear, galloping like a horse.

Without thinking, for no reason, Garson Thayer groped the dashboard and turned the car's faintly whirring heater off. He didn't want distraction, thought he might be able to hear the drumbeat of the bear's paws on the asphalt, hear the animal pant as it galumphed and loped, with surprising grace, astonishing speed and power, down the black band that vanished into the vertical lines of the forest. A bear in motion is practically round, a rolling ball of disembowelment.

Instinct said, speed the fuck up, get us out of here, bears mean business and we're on this monster's turf. But Garson backed his engineer boot off the accelerator. He wanted to watch the bear grow in the rear-view mirror's glass TV screen, wanted to see its face.

Undersized murderous black holes over a maw packed with yellow knives. There was some dog-dick town in Alaska called Yellow Knife... or maybe that was Canada, somewhere to the right of here, and slightly south. Maybe some motorist was being stalked by a bear in Yellow Knife, too. Happens all the time, here in the Yukon, stranger. The bear's little round eyes spoke of hard times, hunger, and something darker, deeper.

Garson's brown eyes slipped to the glowing gas gauge. Reassuring needles and dials said three quarters of a tank left and only one hundred and eighty miles to go before the air base. Barely a calibrated microsquare on the Alaskan radar screen. Continent-sized mass of ice, forest, and buried oil glowed green in oscilloscope-shaped instruments in a darkened war room under the tundra.

So he wasn't really in any danger.

'What's this dumb bear going to do, even if he catches up?' Garson thought. 'Pop a claw like a switchblade and use it like a can-opener on unrecycled Detroit steel?'

He slowed to just over forty mph, wanted to figure out how fast an adult male grizzly could lope, rumble, or charge or whatever it is bears do when intent on murder and dinner. He was fairly sure the bear was male. Females would be busy nursing cubs or telling them bearish bedtime stories.

TV documentary-style slo-mo sequences played in his head. Colossal, practically prehistoric mammals slapped salmon onto dry land as they struggled up waterfalls, enslaved by senseless, suicidal biological imperatives. A bear attacked a wild-eyed moose, felled the ungainly elk like a four-legged tree. Bear locked in life-or-death struggle with a snarling, spitting, raised-fur indignant puma, the animal equivalent of Mexican wrestling. Garson looked in the rear-view mirror again. Obviously, everything he thought he knew about bears was strictly showbiz. Just wasn't logical that a bear would chase an automobile with anything like food in mind.

The bear, according to the car's odometer, maintained a steady thirty-eight mph.

Garson wondered if Kentucky Derby thoroughbreds could gallop that fast. Engineer's curiosity overcame him. How long could the bear maintain this insane pace? How much did the critter weigh? Running style better suited to the open plain than extreme low-temperature tarmac. Claws grab the dirt like linebackers' cleats, sprinters' spikes.

If moose, salmon, and mountain goats could only learn to drive, their populations would increase, and all the world's bears would starve to death.

A world without bears wouldn't be much fun, he thought. Playboy bunny stretched out pale, pink, and wiggling in print, sprawled on a snarling bearskin rug. Snobbish guardsmen in preposterous towering headgear. Northwest Indian shaman dancing a slow frug at the prow of an aircraft-carrierly war canoe, decked out in a bear costume with cartoonish wooden eyes and claws. Garson could practically hear the roar and growl of the Bear Dance chant.

The GI consultant transport vehicle wasn't equipped with an external temperature gauge. Freeze-ass cold was as precise an estimate as Garson Thayer could figure. The car wasn't quite a refrigerator on the inside yet. That could be fixed. On an impulse, steadying the steering wheel with his knees, he reached back and grabbed the dorky green snorkel-coat parka from the car floor.

A parka next to every seat, but no stewardesses on the plane out. No pretty, chatty women handing out joke-sized exact miniature replicas of popular brand booze-bottles. Near-empty C-5A cargo plane contained bleary faces going over blueprints, or dozing, snoring. Ocean of white rolling by below. The occasional snowed-over farms had given way to agriculturally inappropriate prairie, then a jagged mountain range.

He shimmied into the ugly Army-Navy Store wrap, then rolled down the windows. The fur in his nostrils froze instantly.

A lightning-charged oil slick of cold and blackness barged into the car's cockpit. He leaned into the mirror's viewpoint, saw a grey-furred greenish oaf-thing, its facial features obscured. He checked the coat's pockets to see if GI extreme cold weather gear included complimentary OD mittens. Negative mittens. Negative mukluks.

After a few minutes, Garson couldn't feel his fingers or toes. Goddamn engineer boots may look tough and hold up on oily gas station surfaces, but separated from motorcycle engines, they insulate not.

He didn't want to roll up the windows. That'd be cheating. The bear got warmer as he ran. Hot bear-blood coursed full-speed through veins and arteries the diameter of a man's legs. Blood launched in the search for bloody fuel in the battle for life earned through death. Windows open and frozen foot on accelerator seemed fair enough. Give the bear a chance to prove his primitive point. Garson wasn't about to stop the car, get out and run for it, though. Wouldn't be fair to himself. Just hope the engine doesn't overheat and seize up right now.

"Scuse me, Mister Bear, sir, but would you mind waiting while I fix this flat tire? Maybe give the tire-iron a swat to loosen up them lug-nuts, all frozen stiff? Then we can resume the chase on an equal footing.'

Flat tire would be a serious problem. I'd definitely roll up the windows, then. Maybe turn the heater back on. Be okay till the gas runs out. Why can't the motherfucking US Gov't put some CB radio or even a goddamn walkie-talkie in their stupid courtesy cars for non-military consultants? And why don't non-military personnel snorkel coats contain complimentary .45 automatic ordnance?

Garson Thayer had the knowledge and skills to rewire a car radio into a crude communication device with his eyes closed and one hand tied behind his back. But engineering parlour-tricks would be hard to perform with frozen hands and no soldering iron. The car's dashboard cigarette lighter was AWOL. Pocketed as a souvenir, perhaps. Maybe the thing was embossed with cool regimental colours, or a plastic screaming war eagle.

'Help,' he said, as though there were someone around to listen. 'Help. I'm being chased by a bear.'

Sounded like a joke.

Incompletely remembered smutty story about a bear who sodomises an incompetent hunter in retaliation for getting part of his left ear shot off. 'You don't really come here to hunt, do you?'

The bear's face was reduced to a gleam from undersized black beady eyes. Evil marbles, midget demonic eight balls, the black spheres that mean 'you lose', reflecting lunatic lunar glint.

Wasn't physically possible for a bear to run that fast, that long. Not a *human* bear. Not, that is, a regular mammalian super-predator that belonged to planet Earth. 'So maybe I'm seeing things.'

The radars at the air base had been seeing things too. The job he was on involved uninvited blips that came a bit too close to the missile silos, invisible to the naked eye or regular-spec binoculars. The mystery-blips plainly were *not* where the high-taxpayer-dollar radar-scopes reported them to be.

Gov't defence contractors routinely deliver faulty top-secret product at inflationary rates. Which meant there had to be a separate high-clearance budget for non-military consultants with no known conflicts of interest. No radar in the car. No blip on non-radar would mean the bear wasn't real and he, Garson Thayer, had gone foaming, snow-blind nuts.

Slow down a bit more and you'll find out just how real this grizzly is, all over you. Bears tend to gnaw faces off first.

He heard the bear's near-subsonic pant – roar – woof. Accelerated to stay slightly ahead. Checked the mirror. 'Real enough for me.'

Dogs bark, chickens cluck, elephants trumpet, lions roar. Maybe bears roar too. He tried to remember if he'd ever heard bear recordings, like whale songs, birdcalls. As far as he knew, bears snuffled and grunted like pigs, moaned like disappointed hillbillies. He tried impressions of bear-noises. Became, in his shaggy snorkel coat, a bear impersonator.

Garson had to check himself out in the mirror. Raised his right hand from the steering wheel, adjusted the angle, kept it so he could keep an eye on the bear still running inexhaustibly behind.

'Wwwooooorg!' he roared. 'Rawwww!'

No spark of recognition in the furrily inscrutable murder-face outside, or in the less furry one reflected in the mirror. Garson was obviously a failure at incorporating bear spirit. He wasn't the reincarnation of the Haida tribe bear-clan shaman in the Natural History Museum. Maybe the mirror was the problem. He wasn't *facing* the lumbering monster correctly. He could only bear to gaze at the horror in reflection. He was a coward who showed fear. Big mistake, in the wild kingdom.

Took great delicacy of touch and balance to keep his right foot on the accelerator while steering with his left butt-cheek. Garson Thayer leaned out the driver's side window as far as he could go, yelled bear-like incantations, flapped his arms.

The bear took this as an invitation to bare fangs and blare like an Allosaurus. The sonic shock waves nearly tumbled Garson from his precarious lean on the car door. The bear said, don't get cute. I'm going to tear you apart and eat you when I catch you. Chomp your hands and feet off with my bear-trap jaws... *after*

I devour your ugly face, that is. That's so you won't bleed out too fast. Want you alive when I rip your abdomen for vitamin-saturated liver.

Garson was rattled as he read the rampaging relentless bear's innermost vital thoughts. The stronger animal needed food to stay strong. The weaker animal was weaker, and he was there.

'So alls I got to do,' Garson thought, 'is give up this dumb game, forget the dumb rules I made up, take this V8 beast up to a perfectly sane sixty mph and that's all she wrote. What's the dividend in giving ravening carnivores a fighting chance?'

He watched a mental car disappear into due-north darkness, heard imaginary tires screech with sudden pick-up. Thwarted predator groans, slows, drops to its drogue hindquarters to lick seriously sore, badly scraped footpads and, as a consolational afterthought, its genitals. Fantasy bear abandons the asphalt to which its paws are evolutionarily unsuited, stumble-rolls into the woods and dematerialises, a ghostly animal spirit. Real-life bears, resigned to the loss of a protein-intensive, vitamin A-rich gorefeast, settle for substitute dinner of foraged dried blueberries scraped up from under a crust of snow.

'Or else,' Garson thought further, 'speed up *drastically*, pull a U-turn and charge the goddamn bear. Flip the game around. See how he likes them eggs.'

Cartoon bear gapes, stretches beady eyes in goofy, wide-eyed, night-vision surprise. Scene explodes into a swirling smoke-ring mandala. Dazed bear, crumpled car, driver thrown into a nearby tree, one of the smoking wreck's tires still crookedly spinning. The end. Near-forgotten rifle game in the penny arcade of a dingy Luna Park pier on a shore across the continent. Toy shotgun chained to the sad fun-machine's chassis to prevent theft and subsequent no-fun-at-all armed robbery scenarios with the purloined adult toy. Mechanical hillbilly chased by a clockwork black bear. Hit the mirror on the bear's ribcage and the tables turn. 'Why you honey-suckin' varmint! I'll learn ya to eat my sister's panties hangin' on the laundry line.'

Quick engineer-style mental calculation of how the turnaround-is-fair-play tactic would play out in real life. Several tons of cold-rolled steel at sixty-five mph slam headlong into a ton of hot-blooded flesh and bone charging at thirty-eight mph equals dead or badly injured human when ribcage explodes forward into steering column. Massive collateral damage to Gov't Property vehicle and maybe a dead bear, if the monster bruin is in fact made of mortal flesh.

Bears eat carrion. *This* bear would lick blood, brain tissue, and bone marrow off the twisted metal wreckage. Change-of-direction sneak attack wasn't a viable plan.

'The bear's reached his terminal velocity,' Garson thought. '*He* can't seem to go any faster. I can, whenever I feel like it. Probably won't run out of gas or overheat or blow a tire. Road surface is level, well maintained, and was built expressly to lead to the top-secret air base. I can't get lost. All I have to do is stay on the road.'

Stay on the road. Don't go haywire in response to danger-hallucinations. Don't skid off into the trees and crash into a hidden terminal moraine of glacier-shoved boulders. Panting hard, steaming, the bear approaches to investigate. Agony sound effects issue from the ruined broken glass-strewn cockpit. Broken teeth, mouth full to overflowing with blood. Blood from deep gash in scalp floods eyes to stain the hideous scene red as a martyrdom-themed rose window in a Gothic cathedral.

'Just keep going. Keep steady. Maybe speed up a smidge.'

Garson Thayer flicked the high-beams lever, thought he perceived smudgy brown sky glow ahead. Wondered if they'd built the air base in a pre-existent clearing, or if they'd eradicated primordial forest to build the air base. Defoliants, napalm, atomic bulldozers... the US Gov't was invasive on an inhuman scale, even in extreme environments.

The car was hit by and flooded with light. A searchbeam.

Dazzled, Garson fought the instinctual urge to swerve, evade. Light cancelled his view of road, rear-view mirror and the lumbering death machine that chased him. Darkness and safety were left or right, even if there was no road in those directions. No road means you take your chances, even at moderate speed. The light suffused the snorkel coat with cold-sweat heat. The light showed people bathed in light. Garson had heard about this sort of thing. The light meant you were enjoying a near-death experience. The stories were true.

Among the light-angels was Rebecca Raven, a girl he liked in High School. Leukaemia took her young and heartbreakingly beautiful, but spared her virginity. There were many glamorous dazzling faces he didn't recognise, people in the light, like him. They were happy and they were dead, staring at the sun, even though staring at the sun's against the rules, as any kid knows. The rules were wrong. It's wonderful and miraculous to stare into the sun. Got to remember that. Remember to forget the rules. The rule of the sun is, there are no other rules. I alone am the rule and the way into the light.

The blinding sun suddenly developed a deafening voice.

'Attention! Halt! Stop your vehicle! Prepare to be identified!'

'Vehicle,' Garson said, or thought he said. 'Can't stop the vehicle. If I stop the vehicle, the bear will catch, tear, and eat me.'

'Repeat!' the light's voice said. 'Stop your vehicle! You must be recognised! If you do not halt immediately, we will open fire. Flash your lights if you *are unable* stop your vehicle. We'll shoot out your tires.'

The voice sure had a lot to say. If only the voice wouldn't bark quite so metallically. Orders are easier to obey when spoken soothingly. The sun spoke silently, radiated its message of universal love. Rebecca Raven looked so beautiful and *not* dead, in solar heaven.

The windshield exploded into a galaxy-shaped spiderweb without a sound. Then the sound hit, ear-, night-, and light-splittingly.

'Holy shit!' Garson Thayer realised the situation. US Gov't Air Base, missiles, strategic bombers, buzz-cut maniacs with automatic weapons, seriously bored and eager for action in their enforced isolated hibernation. He stomped the brakes to stop the vehicle, as directed. Absurdly heavy car screeched and fishtailed on the frosted arctic highway, but eventually obeyed the voice and halted.

But, the bear. Garson frantically tried to roll up the windows on either side, windmilling like a panic-stricken spastic.

'Please leave your windows in the 'down' position, sir. And we need you to please keep your hands where we can see them.'

He saw the bear snap off his hands, saw the blood spray. Trapped in the vehicle, he could only slap at the bear's snout with slender spurting wrist-stumps. Fear and horror stole his voice. He muttered please please don't eat me as he died.

The MPs took in a shuddering 3D snorkel coat that moaned, '... Eat me... eat me.'

They kept their M16s trained. 'Been drinking, sir?' Booze would've lent the scene a certain logic. The Alaskan landscape encouraged heavy drinking, in undisciplined souls.

Garson Thayer wanted a drink, badly. Water, of the clear, unfrozen kind. He was suddenly flooded with the *all right* feeling, even though uniformed men had their rifles pointed at his hood. Assault rifles potentially as deadly, though considerably quicker, less painful and gruesome, than a grizzly assault.

'Grizzly bear chase me. Grisly bear try kill me,' he said. 'Bad part is... I *let* him. To see what he could do, see? Wanted to see if he'd give up and go away. Only he never did.'

'Bears *have* been reported in the area, sir. Like coyotes, stateside. Or dogs. They tend to chase cars. Don't know what to do once they've caught them, though. Ain't it always that way?' But the MP didn't lower his machine gun.

The other MP said, 'We need to see your ID and orders, please, sir. Locate and deliver them slowly.'

Garson returned to the world, its rarefied military dimension, and complied. 'I *haven't* been drinking, by the way. There *was* a bear.'

The MP lowered his rifle, accepted the non-military personnel ID card. Garson had let his hair grow quite a bit since the picture was taken. Might be a problem. He hadn't thought that far ahead.

'Please pull down your hood... sir. Nice and slow, that's right.'

Garson Thayer let himself be recognised. One of the MPs returned to the guard cabin and ticked off his name and serial number on an aluminium clipboard in the greenish light of the base.

The other MP lowered his M16, stood erect, saluted limply. 'Got to watch out in these parts, sir. Nobody's ever more than about, uh... two hundred miles from a bear, in Alaska.' He raised his hands like claws, bared his teeth and growled. 'But we're on the job, sir. Making the world safe for democracy.'

Garson Thayer returned the salute, resisted the urge to twist the guy some fuck-you hand jive. The world was a place where men had jobs to do. The guard was only doing his job. Garson's job was to inspect highly classified radar equipment that showed objects moving through forbidden airspace that obviously weren't there. On his way to work, he'd been chased by a bear. Armed military police had shot out his windshield. So now he had to stick his head out the window to steer the car, which wasn't his, towards the non-military personnel barracks indicated by yellow-black reflective signs. He looked into the side-view mirror and watched the air base's main gate roll closed.

Nobody captures the realities, mundanities, and psychological challenges of modern life quite like Matt Plass, who is making his fourth Fiction Desk appearance with this story.

Next to Godliness

Matt Plass

A new message on the kitchen chalkboard:

Gotta rush. Can you put rubbish out? xx

Mary's washed the dishes; a concession, perhaps. And two kisses at the end of the note. In the kickbin I find a chunky block of newspaper bound with sticky tape: my broken wine glass made safe for the bin man. I've also *gotta rush*, but I haul the black plastic sacks to the curb. To do otherwise would be a declaration of war.

That evening, as I hang my jacket, Mary meets me in the hallway, wearing her let's try again face.

'Well, thank you,' she says.

'What for?'

'You cleaned the kitchen.'

'All I did was put the rubbish out.' But when I go to the sink for a glass of water, I notice how the chrome taps glint and the granite worktop shines.

Mary heads for bed after the news. We go at different times these days.

'Join me and read?' she says.

'You seen my book?'

Mary shrugs.

'I left it on the armchair.'

'Sorry.'

My whole body remembers the book splayed open on the arm of the chair. It isn't by the bay window, or next to the toilet, or in any of my other reading roosts. I find it back on the bookshelf, lodged between an unread Dickens and an unread Dawkins.

I open a bottle of wine and chalk a note on the blackboard:

Forget you tidied my book? Or is this another comment on my housework?

Next morning, the Mary-leaving-the-house sounds are sharper than usual. I wait for the slam of the front door before I venture down for coffee. My note has been erased and another chalked in its place:

What comment would I be making exactly?

That evening we have plans, but Mary texts me as I leave work: she has stomach ache. I walk into the Turk's Head alone. Louise and Phil already have a pint on the bar for me. Louise smiles. Phil smiles. 'How are you bearing up?' Phil asks. After one gulp I know I'll be in there till closing.

I wake late, find my clothes pooled on the landing where I must have shed them the night before. In the kitchen I find a message:

I'm worried about you.

My mouth is too dry for toast. I take the coffee jar from the cupboard above the fridge and prepare a flask for the car. At the front door I stop, lay down my bag and walk back into the kitchen, back to the cupboard above the fridge. I'd seen-it-but-not-seen it when I took down the coffee. Our cupboard, usually a refugee camp for displaced food items, is now a shopkeeper's dream. Every jar and packet is aligned. Rows of canned tomatoes and black-eyed beans stand to attention on parade, labels facing front, perfect as a supermarket shelf.

Where's the chalk?

I underline the last word in Mary's note and add an exclamation mark:

I'm worried about you!

Work drags. I'm still 'poor Chris' in the office. It's exhausting.

At six, I find Mary in the kitchen, rubbing the curve of her back against the lip of the sink.

'Just a few beers,' I say. 'Don't pull that face. I'm on top of it.'

Mary pulls out the cutlery drawer and leaves it hanging like a wooden tongue. She moves along the wall, feet shuffling like a ballet dancer as she opens each cupboard one by one. Everything is a picture of order. The cupboards are pristine; all of them, not just the one I saw this morning. And the cutlery drawer: knives with knives, spoons with spoons, forks with forks, blades and scoops and tines gleaming.

'Very neat,' she says.

'I noticed.'

'Not exactly us, though, is it?'

We watch each other. After a while I say, 'Mary, after what happened to us last year, doesn't this make a kind of sense?'

She exhales. Relief, I think. 'Yes,' she says. 'I suppose it does.'

'Restoring order. Retaking control.'

'Exactly.'

And we smile at each other.

'I knew it wasn't the alcohol,' she says. 'You've upped your unit count, but you're not daytime drinking and the cutlery wasn't this way when I left for work. This happened today; after

I'd gone. What I'm saying is, perhaps you might want to chat with Dr Bowman. He might have a perspective on this kind of thing.'

This takes a moment to slide through the workings of my brain.

'You think it was me who rearranged the kitchen,' I say.

That night we eat our lamb casserole in silence. I chew cubes of dead meat and think back to our sessions with Dr Bowman, his humourless eyes pinning us to the corduroy sofa. 'You should expect the unexpected. Loss manifests in myriad, oftentimes bizarre, ways.'

Watching Mary clear her plate, something softens in me. In her too, I guess, because later, in bed, for the first time in a long time, we reach for each other.

Saturday morning we breakfast in companionable silence. Mary washes up, then walks into town to secure jam jars from charity shops. Today, she will make chutney for Christmas gifts. I'll take the trail bike up onto the hills. We still do stuff, you see.

Halfway up the savage incline of Ditchling Rise, I pedal past a suited man and a young girl in a purple coat. They crouch at the edge of Stanmer Wood, absorbed in something on the ground. It's a girl-sized bow and Dad has an arrow in his hand. She takes the string with two fingers, the way she's been shown. Dad shadows her arms with his own; together they sight and draw and release. The arrow wobbles through the air and lodges crossways in the branches of a tree. 'I hunted the tree. It works, Daddy, it works.'

Three minutes later I find myself at the top of Ditchling Rise, leant over the handlebars with the Devil howling in my chest and acid in my blood.

Back at the house a new bottle of bleach sits on the kitchen counter, but I don't expect Mary back till noon. I call out her name.

Then I see the chalkboard. *I cleaned upstairs. I'm so sorry.*

The *y* of sorry has a curly tail that I haven't seen before.

I'm halfway up the stairs when I notice that the door we don't open, the one to the bedroom we don't go in, hangs ajar.

And inside, yes, order has been restored. My Alicia's bed is made; even the precious dent in the pillow has been plumped. Her books are back on the packing case in height order, right to left. The carpet is bare of toys and colouring pencils. Three pairs of shoes that should be scattered now peek out in a single neat row from below the duvet hem. The wicker chair is bereft of strewn clothes. I know that if I open the wardrobe, I'll find Alicia's school uniform, pressed and hung.

Below me, the front door lock clicks. Mary's voice carries up the stairs, wondering where I am. Before I can answer, her footsteps are on the stair.

'How could you?' It's all I can say.

Mary pushes me aside and flings herself onto the end of the tiny bed, pulling toys from a plastic box-tidy. She waves a cloth rabbit at me. 'This one. Where was this one? Where *exactly*?'

I start to ask when she did this, why she did this, but Mary is on her feet and pounding at my chest with her fists. I try to fold her in my arms but she wriggles under my elbow and flees down the hall. The key turns in the bathroom door. I probe my chest with two fingers, a bruise forming over my lungs.

At the bathroom door. 'What's in your head, Mary? Talk to me.'

Through the wood, her voice sounds pre-recorded, distant. 'How dare you go in there? How dare you mess with her things?'

'Mary, you know it wasn't me. Talk to me, Mary.'

'You! It was you! It was you!'

'Mary, it wasn't. You know it wasn't. I swear. Please come out. Please come out and talk to me.'

The door stays closed. In the kitchen I boil a kettle three times before I remember to pour water into the waiting mug. I'll call Bowman in the morning.

Mary appears in the doorway, dressing gown over her day clothes. 'Swear it wasn't you,' she says.

'You know it wasn't.'

'Promise it wasn't you?'

I slap the table and shout something red and stupid. Mary just stands in the doorway, frowning. Then she's back up the stairs and I hear the clunk of the bathroom lock. An hour later, Mary returns to the kitchen. This time she walks past me to the kettle and busies herself with tea-making.

'I have not opened that door for months,' I say, in the voice I've been rehearsing.

Mary nods. She fetches a mug from the cupboard. 'I believe you,' she says. Her hand-movements are sharp and accurate, the way they move when she draws.

'Mary, will you tell me what's in your head?'

Mary flips her teabag into the sink and joins me at the table, the mug a source of warmth in her cupped hands. 'So that wasn't you, either?' she says, pointing to the message on the chalkboard with the curly-tailed *y*.

I cleaned upstairs. I'm so sorry.

'No, not me.'

'Ah,' she says.

'Ah, what?'

'I suppose,' she says, 'that if I'm honest, I've felt it for weeks.'

'Okay.'

'The kitchen cleaning. Your book. The kitchen cupboards. The cutlery drawer. Now Alicia's room.'

'Okay.'

Mary leans over and places her hand over mine. 'You feel it?'

'Feel what?'

Mary whispers, 'She's still with us.'

'Oh, no.'

No, no, no, no.

'She's trying to help,' says Mary. 'She wants to be a good girl. Look at you, you think I'm losing my mind, but I feel her. You say it isn't you; I know it's not me. Who else could it be? I feel like getting drunk. Have we any fizzy wine?'

'Drink your tea,' I say.

Later, with Mary asleep on the sofa, I step outside to call Dr Bowman. He's polite for a man taking a business call on a Saturday night. On the way up to bed, I tell her we have an appointment Monday morning.

'Whatever you want, honey,' she says.

Monday morning, I climb out of sleep to the sounds of the shower. Mary and I meet in the hall. She is wrapped in two towels, one fastened above her breasts, the other around her hair.

'Our appointment's not till eleven,' I say.

Mary removes toothpaste from the corner of her mouth. 'Do you think we should redecorate? Winnie the Pooh is young for a seven-year-old, no? I'm sure she'd prefer something a little more sophisticated.' Mary disappears into our bedroom. Underneath the whir of the hairdryer I hear what might be singing. In the shower I rehearse my lines, but when I exit the bathroom Mary is already at the front door, checking her hair.

'Mary?'

'It's nearly eight. I'm late for work.'

'What about our appointment?'

'Bowman? He'll only lecture, or give me pills.'

'I'd like his opinion.'

'You go see him, then. I don't need Bowman's opinion. I know what I know.' She turns and looks up the stairs to where I stand half-naked. 'Aren't you excited,' she says, 'to see what she does next?'

You always assume that, if you needed to, you could hide in your own home. But after Mary has left, I find no alcove large enough to obscure a grown man with a camera; no cupboard with sufficient crawlspace. In the end I sit on the toilet with the lid down, the bathroom door open a fraction of an inch, ready to capture Mary when she reaches the top stair. I need proof; for her, not for me.

I wait twenty minutes before the scrape of the back door tells me I was right. From downstairs comes the whump of a bag hitting the kitchen counter, running water as a bucket is filled, followed by the scratch of chalk on the chalkboard, footsteps that begin sharp then soften as floorboards give way to hall carpet. I hear the creak of the second stair; the creak of the fifth. These are light steps. Lighter even than Mary's dancer's tread. Light enough to belong to a child?

I press record on the camera and watch the landing on the two-by-two display. The footsteps reach the landing. Too soft. Too soft for Mary. They reach my hiding place. The edge of our red mop-bucket glides into view, followed by the hem of a polka dot skirt, followed by –

I close my eyes and when I open them, the footsteps have moved into our bedroom. The radio comes on. The intruder whistles to a Christmas song. I'm on my feet, aching to know. The landing is empty, our bedroom door is closed.

'Alicia?' I say as I push at the bedroom door.

A woman in her fifties kneels by the bed, her back to me, scrubbing at a wine stain on the carpet. She's tiny, with dirty blonde hair tied behind her head. She's wearing Marigolds.

I say, 'It's red wine. You won't get it out. We tried.'

The woman drops her cloth and gasps, one hand clapped to her heart as if to hold it in. Pale, oval eyes peer from deep sockets. 'Oh, my,' she says in a raspy girlish voice. 'I didn't know you were in.' She pushes herself to her feet, and folds the cloth neatly over the rim of the bucket. 'When you call the police,' she says, 'tell them it's Georgie Kemp. It saves time and they'll be less cross. I've taken nothing, just so as you know. Is that thing on?'

I lower the camera. 'Mary sent you?'

'I'm afraid not.'

'Then what is this?'

The woman sighs. 'This,' she says, 'is what I do. By the way, I didn't break anything getting in. Key under the flowerpot, second place I looked. And I've never taken a penny. I even bring my own cleaning products. I'm so sorry about your daughter's room.'

'You know about Alicia?'

Georgie Kemp screws her knuckles into her eyes. 'Idiot, Georgie! I knew there was sadness here, but I didn't make the connection till I'd finished the room. By then it was too late. Was Mary very upset?'

'She thinks Alicia is alive. Not alive, but here; with us.'

'Oh, my. Are you going to call the police?'

'I don't know. I might. Right now, I'm going to put the kettle on. You'd better come down.'

I let her pass, follow her broad back along the landing. Georgie Kemp has the lock-legged stride of someone who spends too much time on her knees. On the chalkboard are new words: *Take heart, Mary*. The Y in Mary has a curly tail.

'Shall I make it?' she says. 'I know where everything is.'

I wave her into a chair.

'You're right,' she says. 'That would be weird.'

Georgie takes her tea black with two sugars. She has rolling tobacco but I ask her to wait until she's outside. When I prompt her, Georgie tells me about the first time: a front door left open in Prentice Street, too inviting to resist, and inside a kitchen floor that had never met a mop. How often does she do it? Oh, all the time; she's always on the look for new clients. It never lasts, you see. The family twigs; no one believes in the cleaning fairy. And she has this terrible habit of leaving notes. I ask about the police and she tells me they were unpleasant the first time, responding to what they thought was a robbery in progress. Kinder the second time: a conversation not interrogation, a doctor not an officer.

'They gave me a fancy word for what I have,' she says. 'I only know this calms my heart. Buys me space and time. I used to be a different person, chaotic. I broke stuff. But now... I leave things better than I find them.'

Georgie asks about Alicia and I tell her, though there's not much to tell: Alicia was here for exactly long enough to reshape every atom in Mary and I. Then one day she stepped into a busy road and forgot to look left.

We talk about Mary. Georgie, who knows us through our chalkboard, is confident we'll make it; she has faith in the human capacity to make things right. We forget the time. Mary's key in the lock makes us both start. Georgie asks if she should go.

'No, I need you to stay.'

Mary steps into the kitchen. She smiles vaguely at Georgie and places two tester paint pots on the table.

'I think Whistle Stone Blue,' she says. 'It's clean and creamy. Alicia will adore it.'

I watch Mary rummage in the cupboard under the stairs for a paint brush. In a moment I will help her out of her coat, sit her down, and bring her tea. Then, with Georgie's help, I will take from Mary, for the second time, the one thing no one can afford to lose.

Tamsin Hopkins is making her Fiction Desk debut with this story, in which a family is troubled not by skeletons in the cupboard but rather ghosts at the table...

The Table

Tamsin Hopkins

'And to the twins I leave my grandmother's table, at which they have spent so many happy hours and which has done so much to enable their creativity.'

Sarah objected. 'Was she losing it at the end, Dad? And we didn't notice?'

'No, pet. She was okay.'

My sister cried then. She had arrived late and had missed our mother's last hours. She could have made it, if she'd taken notice of my texts, emails, messages on every phone I could think of, but oh no, it was, 'Why didn't somebody let me know? I'll never forgive myself for missing the end. Oh, oh, oh.' No thought about what I should have been doing, instead of trying to get hold of her.

We weren't having a big reading of the will or anything like that, no leather armchairs with lawyers telling us what we'd all got, who had been snubbed and who had been elevated. Anyway, my mum wasn't like that. It was just us sitting round the table: me, Dad, and now that she'd arrived, Sarah. Our brother Drew was out doing some errands but wouldn't be long. Unless he took one of his detours.

Mum had been ill for almost a year and she had already given us all the things she wanted us to have. The rest was Dad's. Nothing to it. Except the big table and chairs. *Granny's Curse* she called it as a kind of joke, because although the set was elegant, it was enormous. Too heavy and too long for the kind of room my parents could afford, it belonged in a stately home; still, her grandmother had made her promise to look after it. For years my parents lived in studios and flats that were hardly bigger than the table, which meant squeezing between the high-backed chairs and the wall to get to the fridge and having to pay people to carry it up stairs that were too narrow, or to get it through windows which had to be removed first; all of which cost more than they could afford, especially when they were young. The table didn't go with any of their other furniture either. It looked ridiculous with a portable telly and bunny ears perched down one end and the futon almost underneath it, but still she wouldn't sell it or let Dad saw the legs off to get it down the hall. She said it was too ornate and nobody would have paid much for it anyway, but that wasn't the reason.

Mum told me there had once been a whole bedroom set in the same wood, walnut we thought, with double armoire, a massive sled bed, two chests and matching bedside tables, but at least she had managed to turn that down. By the end, her granny, my great-grandmother, had also lived in a tiny apartment with all that furniture packed round her, like a belligerent squirrel holed up against a winter she would not survive. She could never have afforded to buy such furniture, so the story goes. There were various theories, but she had been in service in her girlhood and we thought it must have come to her through that connection, although nobody knows how or why; she told so many versions of her past that we disregarded them all. The table had been important though, part of my mother's childhood, and she had a strong attachment to it, which was why it had figured so much in our childhood.

We were sitting at that table looking at Mum's papers and letters, including the will. My sister had stopped crying. She looked at Dad with red eyes.

'She's left the table to the twins? What twins?'

Nobody said anything.

'So... what, Dad? She had twins before she met you and gave them up for adoption or something?'

'No pet. We were young, and she hadn't had any babies.'

'But you wouldn't know. You hear about it all the time. The birth mother gives them up out of necessity, or maybe shame in those days. Lives a different life after that, in denial until, bam! The child exercises its legal right to find the birth mother.'

'No Sarah. It wasn't that.'

'What, then? I mean –'

'What are we going to do about the will?' I cut in. 'Is it a real will? Perhaps we don't have to actually do anything.'

'Well, Mr Busswald will have a look at it anyway, and then we'll take it from there,' he said.

'Dad... these are those twins, aren't they?' I said after a while.

'Yes, pet. I expect so.' He didn't meet my eye; I looked at him and he seemed much more frail now, his skin translucent, his movement all brittle sinew. He took his glasses off and pressed his eyes for a moment, then he put them back on and went into the kitchen to make tea. Despite us, he was alone for the first time in forty-five years.

Sarah thumped her feet up onto one of the chairs.

'She must have been losing it at the end,' she said when he'd gone. 'Probably the drugs.' She sniffed, raking through her cavernous sack of a handbag for a tissue. I passed her one of mine from my sleeve. The snot would hit her kids' shoes before she found anything in that bag. Children are a gift, but they are not always given to the most deserving.

She sniffed again. 'When did Drew leave?'

'Just before you got here. He'll be back.'

Our brother had made it up from London, in time for Mum's last hours. He'd go back there soon, back to his wife and kids and put us out of his mind.

'Where's he gone?'

'The flowers.'

'Ooh, I'd think you'd do that.'

'Or you could,' I said.

'Is he alright? I mean, you don't think he'll go "off the rails" again or anything?' she made inverted commas with her fingers.

'No, Sarah. He seems fine.'

She got up and surveyed the sideboard, picking up Mum's things, her clock, the figurines, turning them upside down as if she might suddenly discover something valuable.

'How come you know what it's about? The twin thing? Nobody tells me anything.'

'You don't listen,' I told her.

'You don't say anything,' she said.

Actually that's true, because as soon as she knows anything, she uses it against you. I learned the hard way with her. Anyway, Sarah does know what twins Dad is talking about, I know she does. They were a feature of our childhood. Mallory and Meg they were called. Drew remembers; Dad read the will to him before he went out. He laughed and said Mum had always had a sense of humour.

Mallory and Meg, the twin girls in school uniform, with long plaits on either side of their heads that fell forwards as they worked and which they flicked back periodically. Sometimes, when the plaits were too annoying, they would tie the ends together so they wouldn't fall forward into the paint or get in the clay. They had navy blue pinafore dresses like at my junior school, with pleated skirts and a white blouse on underneath. I never saw them in any other clothes. They were always deep in concentration, sat at the big table, never saying much but they would look up together and smile at you and then get back down to work.

They didn't come to school with us or come into the garden to play, but when you did your homework, there they were, ruling off the margins neatly and writing the date at the top of each page like we were supposed to do but never did.

We knew, had always known, that Mallory and Meg were connected to my mother; this was never questioned or even discussed as far as I remember. Dad never mentioned it, although he smiled at them when he brought his tea and paper to the table. And they smiled back. Everything happened at the table; there was nowhere else. Our little house was too small and the table too big.

After my brother was born, my mother was told it would be unwise for her to have any more babies. They couldn't afford more anyway. I thought she furnished herself with an extra set of children after that: spares, or wished for daughters that she wanted so much that she dreamt them, imagined them, until they were real. They were just a fact of life, even when we had someone to tea. If someone sat at the table at Mallory's place or pulled up a chair so Meg had to move her books out of the way, they moved without any fuss. Most kids didn't take any notice. Most kids naturally chose another place; after all, there were plenty, the table was so big. There was just this one girl who used to make things awkward, a friend of Sarah's known to Drew and me as Beverly Rabbit, because of her teeth. 'Can I sit here?' she'd say, looking exaggeratedly at the place. 'Is one of them in this chair?' But Mallory and Meg would just tut to each other, raise their eyebrows and get on with their painting or their jigsaw. Beverly Rabbit liked to say 'Shall we play musical chairs?' Then she and Sarah would snigger into their juice as Mum was passing out the fish fingers.

Mallory and Meg didn't go upstairs. They liked to work at the table. You could have friends in your bedroom to play music, or to snog when the parents were out, and since there was never any fuss about them, you got so you didn't notice if they were there or not. When you charged down to breakfast and put your blazer on with a slice of toast in your mouth, they were probably there, and if we ordered in pizza and had it on the floor in front of the telly, they didn't join in so maybe they were there and maybe they were somewhere else. I don't suppose I thought about them at all, once I went to college.

Dad came back in with the tea on a big tray that was too heavy for him. Sarah immediately put down a little shepherd girl she had been examining and moved towards him, hovering. She thought he was going to drop the tea, and so did I. He teetered a little, trying to put the tray down without everything sliding forward, but then he got it and we let out our breath. The doorbell went: Drew was back.

'I was thinking about it in the car,' he said and pulled out a chair to sit on. 'The table and that. I mean, it always gets passed to the women.' He ran his fingers along the grain.

'That's right,' said Dad, now handing out the cups.

'Go on, Dad,' I said.

'Go on nothing. It's a woman's thing, that's all.'

'What is?' said Sarah.

'That's just what I mean,' Drew said. 'Mum had brothers and so did Gran, but it was the women who got dumped with the table, not the boys.'

'So?'

'So, it's really for you two to sort out between you, I think,' he said nodding at me and Sarah. 'I mean, I think it's got nothing to do with me and they wouldn't want me to have the table anyway, so I shouldn't have to have it. That's all.'

'Who wouldn't want you to have it?' I said.

'I'm not bloody having it,' said Sarah, crossing her arms. 'I mean, it's huge. Where will I put it?'

'I can't fit it in my flat either,' I said.

'Anyway, it's ugly.'

'It's not ugly,' I said. 'You've got no taste for antiques.'

Dad was nodding, looking at the table.

'What d'you reckon, Dad?' said Drew.

'I reckon your mother knew what she was doing, that's what I reckon. Always did. A clever woman that.' He passed round a plate of Bourbon creams.

We ate our biscuits. I brushed imaginary crumbs from my knee and Drew stared out at the garden. Sarah was the first to break the silence.

'What did she know she was doing, Dad?'

He looked at her photo on the sideboard. 'Your mother knew it was difficult to live with. She meant it as a joke, but it *was* a bit of a curse, that table.' He looked out of the window.

'And?' said Sarah.

It took him a few moments to get going again.

'I should have thought it was obvious,' he said. 'She's left it to them. So you don't have to have it now.'

'Eh?'

'I mean, they're not real? Are they?'

'They were real enough to her.' And that was all he would say. He went out into the garden to brush down his bird table and refill the bird bath. We left him to his thoughts.

I stacked the tray and we went into the kitchen together; I did the washing up and Drew looked through the cupboards for something to eat while Sarah flicked a tea towel around.

'S'gonna be takeaway, by the state of these cupboards. Who's for fish and chips?'

'Yeah, great,' said Sarah.

'The thing is,' I said, 'the girls haven't been around for a while. Has anybody seen them?'

'No,' said Drew.

Sarah clucked her tongue. 'Don't be daft,' she said rolling her eyes.

'Hey, don't start!' I said. 'You know you all used to play with them, just like me. Colouring paper doilies and making clay animals, all of us did it. I bet there's still some of their creations in the loft.'

'Oh, for God's sake,' said Sarah.

I felt tears behind my eyes. Drew took my hand. 'Look, Evie, it's all in the past. It's just the will bringing this up again. It'll all blow over soon.'

'You know they were part of our family, just like you and me.'

Sarah was leaning in the doorway.

'Well, not quite like you and me, were they?'

It was true. They hadn't aged, for one thing. And they hardly spoke. I thought of Mum and the tears came in a rush.

Drew hugged my shoulders. 'Look, it's all because we're upset, see. We're all very upset and we want to please Mum and do what she said in the will, but really, what... I mean, how can you leave something to a hallucination?'

'Two hallucinations,' snorted Sarah.

'Okay, but two hallucinations with plaits and a box of watercolours and paintings that actually developed from blank paper to finished works, which Mum framed,' I said.

'Evie, she did them! Isn't it obvious?'

'So, what, are you saying you didn't ever see Meg and Mallory? That you just said you did to please her? Because I can remember you doing clay with them. Don't say I made that up.' I had run out of tissues now. Sarah found hers in the sack bag and passed me the packet.

'Not exactly,' she said. 'But I have thought about it over the years. I think we somehow joined in her visions, because it suited us, or maybe it was some sort of complicit hallucination thing. I don't know. Just to please her maybe.'

'Okay, okay, but listen: do you remember Mum ever, I mean ever, talking about them? I mean telling us what they looked like or describing what they were doing?'

'You're right,' said Drew after a while. He was clearly uncomfortable discussing the whole thing. 'She never told us what to think. She just carried on as if they had always been there, a normal part of the family.'

Dad came back in from the garden. He began decanting peanuts into a plastic tube for the bird feeder and getting more in the sink than into the tube. Drew stood next to him; he found a small scoop and helped to funnel the fat little nuts.

'Dad, who are they? Mallory and Meg?' he said quietly. 'Are they ghosts?'

'The twins,' said Sarah. 'Mum's hallucinations, weren't they?'

Dad put his mottled hands on the edge of the sink and looked out of the window. He seemed more upset than ever. Eventually he looked at Drew.

'No pet,' he said. 'They came with the table.'

Mr Busswald, Dad's old lawyer, says that he doesn't mind if I come and go as much as I please. It suits everybody if I check up on things from time to time. The padlock is stiff, but I get it eventually. I haven't been for a while but everything looks the same. A bit dusty. The girls look up from their painting and wave at me. I wave back and put my bag in the corner. I get my box of paints out and join them at the table. Hi Mallory. Hi Meg. How are you? There are no windows here; most storage units don't have them, although I tried to find one that did. The light is wrong for painting watercolours but that can't be helped, just for now.

I tell the girls what has been happening in the family. Sarah has got divorced, that was a while ago. Sorry I haven't been to see you for so long. Her kids are grown up now so it wasn't too much of a fiasco, although I don't know how her husband put up with her so long. Drew still lives in London, so I don't see them very often either, although I gather everything's going well for them. I've been okay. It was hard when my Frank passed, but I'm getting back to normal now. I just wish we'd had children, but what will be, will be, as the saying goes. Mallory nods. Meg likes the tree I am doing in gouache. It's quite good, even if I say so myself.

Anyway, I tell them, I have a bit more room now. I've had a clear out and I've measured it up: the table will fit in the conservatory, just about. The girls look at me. You could come home with me if you like, I say. I can get some removal men to come and get you, and there's a view of the garden, like before. You would like that, I say. It would be no trouble. What do you think? They look at me and then they put their brushes down and hug each other. It's not for me to say, I tell them. It's your decision. I mean, after all, it's your table.

'The Armies' is the third Fiction Desk story from our resident Slovenian author Miha Mazzini. Several of his novels have been translated into English, and are worth tracking down. Look out for The German Lottery *(CB Editions) and* Crumbs *(Freight Books).*

This story translated by Lenart Pogacnik.

The Armies

Miha Mazzini

A cloud drifted across the sky.

The child latched onto the window with his lips, flattening his nose against the glass. Focusing all of his power into a gaze aimed at the cloud, he ordered it:

'Stop!'

The cloud obeyed. Some wisps wanted to slip away, but the child's gaze caught them in time.

Everything went still. Outside, the heat kept on rising from the courtyard, churning amongst the blocks of apartments. Almost as if it was coming from a blistering barbecue that someone had left unattended for far too long.

Picnics.

The child's gaze drifted through the gaps between the apartment buildings, towards the forest. Smoke trailed from the branches above the nearby river. People from other apartments sat by the water with bottles cooling in their watery cribs made of stones. Everyone was there.

But he had to watch over Grandma. Diligent ten-year-old boys ought to do this with pleasure.

He knew that he should turn around to check up on her, but he couldn't trust the cloud to stay in its place.

'Don't you dare!'

He took a quick glance across the room and towards the corner where Grandma was napping. His eyes refocused on the cloud; it had already begun to move. The traitor.

'I'm not like that,' said the child. 'I wouldn't imprison you. I wouldn't imprison anyone. Go!'

The cloud stretched out and swirled, leaving only the blue sky behind it.

The child listened to Grandma's breathing. Nothing? In his fear he threw himself across the bed, almost reaching the body in the grey-patterned gown. The acrid smell of urine Grandma could no longer control clasped his nostrils.

The bed squeaked and Grandma awoke in panic:

'Ah? Ah?'

'Shhhh... Shhhh...' The child soothed her, and crept back into his corner. His back pressed harder than before against the cold wall and his head tilted back, even though this was forbidden because hair could leave marks on the paint. Droplets of sweat formed on his upper lip. With his half-closed eyes, he noticed the stack of books that he couldn't read anymore, the bedside television that he wasn't allowed to turn on during the day. He embraced his knees with his skinny white arms and focused on his breath, his lips moving into odd shapes. The air, drawn through his teeth, seemed to cool him down. So he sucked it in faster and louder, until Grandma began to breathe uneasily once again. The sweat drenched her headscarf, so the windows had to stay shut. She always said that a combination of fresh air and sweat led to illness.

By looking at the clock, the child began to hear it as well. The mechanism was grinding oddly, as if sticking. Like drops of rain... the river. Picnics. He imagined the coldness of the water cutting into his feet, as if he had stepped on a knife. If Mother came to visit, maybe she could watch Grandma for him. Probably not though. He closed his eyes and tried to concentrate: 'Come, come, come!' But he didn't have any faith in himself. It was too hot and the hollowness was taking hold of him. He didn't know what kind of mood Mother would be in anyway. But if she was happy and if he were to hear her steps, oh! They would echo across the empty apartment building like a pebble in a tin can. After a search for the key inside her bag, the lock would open and Mother would stand there, smiling!

He opened his eyes. She wasn't smiling. He didn't know if he was dreaming.

Mother's eyelids formed sharp slits.

His hollowness was suddenly filled with fear; an icy cramp rose from his belly towards the back of his neck.

He dared not move. The slightest error could bring her wrath. If he moved... if he didn't move... if... if...

She stepped towards him and started puffing, her nostrils trembling like a balloon about to burst. The waves of her breath struck his drenched skin. The sweat ran down the crack between his buttocks, and he couldn't tell whether or not he had just wet himself.

The stillness of their bodies. Mother was not just breathing; she was pumping air into herself, building up pressure. The child bored his way down into the floor and back into the wall, as if his body was a drill.

Mother's left hand gripped the handle of her bag. Her fist whitened and began to shake. She reached for the bag's leather strap, which was biting into her shoulder – Aaaaaahhh – and pulled the bag off, hurling it onto the bed. It bounced and hit Grandma, who began to wave her hands around frantically.

A shower of saliva droplets sprayed the child's face:

'Hello to you too!' said Mother.

Grandma was shouting something, but the child didn't dare look away from Mother's face. The red turned to crimson, the teeth searching for flesh to sink into. This morning, as the three of them had attended the morning mass hand in hand, her face had worn a festive mask. Soft fabrics, smooth features, and curved smiles everywhere. At home, however, the mask fell off. And so did the skin, baring the face down to its flesh, gums and bones, saliva and eyelids.

'Get up!'

Had he leapt up even before she said it?

He didn't even feel the smack.

'Brigitte is a whore, is that clear?'

Which Brigitte?

'Say it!'

'Um...'

Smack.

'Brigitte is a whore.'

'Louder!'

'BRIGITTE IS A WHORE!'

'Are you nuts, why are you shouting? What will the neighbours think!?'

They were trapped in their quiet screaming, as always. The kind where the body prepared for a roar, but the throat constricted to contain all of the voice's power within the walls of the apartment.

He screamed with a tight throat that Brigitte was a whore. Then Mother added that all blondes were whores, and he had to scream this with her.

Grandma finally got to her feet and intervened with whispered screams: 'Leave the child alone! What does he have to do with your man-whores?'

Mother spun around as if on a trigger.

'You! You're the one to talk! You!'

She hissed around the bed into Grandma's corner.

The child slid down the wall, being careful not to touch the paint with his hair.

The blaming, the cursing, and the sound of the first slaps all meant a possible arrival of the Armies. He must be vigilant.

His hands were shaking so much that he had to look down to see if they were his at all. Would he be able to grasp his weapon?

His fingertips began to scratch the baseboard in the corner, moving it out of place.

He no longer had any toys, as ten-year-old boys are too old to have any. But one day when he was watching over Grandma, he had decided to shake that baseboard so hard that its nails gave in. As their heads popped out of their holes, he lured them further into the open by using the flesh of his fingers as bait. They sunk their teeth in, and it hurt, but the nails left their dens and he tossed them into the toilet, flushing it many times afterwards in order to make sure that they would not return.

The child had to get hold of the baseboard so as to arm himself. Years ago, he had noticed how the Armies attacked only during these conversations, as Mother referred to what went on between her and Grandma. First, just a small group of explorers and then, if he failed to fend them off, the main force. Sometimes he drove them off at the last moment, even as they climbed the balcony, banging against the window. That baseboard was his only weapon.

The child hid in his corner and cautiously peeked out of the window and onto the courtyard.

Behind him, he could hear cursing, skin slapping skin, a lock of hair coming loose as one of the women squealed.

The courtyard, a sea of asphalt.

A Roman ship?

Hold fast, my elephants, he said. They have come after us. I should have destroyed Rome when I had the chance.

The board in his hands transformed into a catapult. The fireball it produced struck the vessel amidships and sank it.

Mother pushed Grandma to the floor where she begged for mercy, but due to the furious battle with the Romans, the child did not hear her.

The night was not a cool one. Sweat ran down Grandma's face, blending with the water that dripped from her cold compress. The child sat next to her, looking down at the floor.

'Ohhh, I suffer all this because of you! My God, my God! I could be enjoying a quiet old age, but that bitch just had to give birth and hustle you in here. I don't need this! Let her take care of her own brats! But I'm a good Christian and so I make this sacrifice for you.'

Grandma didn't usually talk directly to him, preferring to complain about him in his presence, about how unnecessary he, and the life he brought with him, was.

But the hint of a smile crossed the child's face. Deep down, he was reliving the last moments of the mighty Roman army, which had turned into a burning mess of floating wooden debris and corpses before being swallowed by the sea.

The teacher dwelled on the child's bruise for a moment, but in the end said nothing. Slovenia is such a tiny nation that secrets must be left not only unsaid, but not turned even into thoughts; otherwise people would have moved away from one another in disgust long ago. Mother had commanded the child to take good care of Grandma's bruises, so they would fade by mass the following Sunday. Just the ones on her face, though: whatever was under her clothes wasn't important.

The child sat at the back of the class and worried about Grandma. When he was five years old, a man had moved into his mother's apartment, and Mother had held the child by his shoulders and said that she trusted him. But he must not fail her trust. A mission awaited him, and he must carry it out. At that moment, he had agreed to move into Grandma's apartment and take care of her, since she was old and weak. That was his duty. Mother had to go to work, so she couldn't do it, but she promised to come as often as possible, at every free moment. He felt strange at these words; he needed to go to the toilet, his stomach was churning. But Mother instantly saw the whirlwind in him. 'I can see you're happy,' she said. 'He who has a mission has a purpose.'

So every day he took care of his school duties quickly, just so he could stare at the wall and take care of Grandma later. Just as he kept waking up during the night to check if Grandma was still breathing, he also tried to travel in his mind into Grandma's apartment during classes, to check if she was still alive.

The school bell rang and the teacher left the classroom. The child's classmates gathered into groups, and the noise expanded like a jellyfish. The child drew tiny lines in his notebook, flinching occasionally as a piece of chalk hit his head. His thoughts were still with Grandma, even though the next class was PE. He was one of those kids that PE teachers marked as 'special' as soon as they set their eyes on them.

Mother was waving a wooden spoon.

'Turn around!' she screamed.

He had hoped that Brigitte would let go of Mother's man so Mother wouldn't be so angry and pay them so many visits. The child turned around and tensed in anticipation of every strike. Grandma would sooner or later intervene and then he would have to watch out for the Armies.

Maybe they were already on their way? What if one day he couldn't win? He never knew what kind of Army would attack, but he recognised them from the movies that he had seen on television. Rarely were the Armies comprised of monsters; those he could deal with easily. It was much harder to combat human Armies, those of the Romans, Huns, Turks, Germans, and cowboys. The child couldn't understand why they attacked only when the women were having a discussion. Once, Grandma had said that the devil works when you're not careful. When he was younger, he couldn't take his eyes off Mother and Grandma's brawls, their arms and heads jerking almost like a dance, but now his attention was diverted to the Armies. We must never allow them to enter, never. We must always gaze outside, onto the courtyard, watching for the Armies.

Burning welts stretched across his backside. Grandma intervened and Mother started quarrelling with her. The child glanced across the balcony. Napoleon's troops were marching. In a panic, he ripped off the baseboard and opened fire upon them. They just kept coming. They had drummers and attacked in orderly, rectangular formations. He unloaded his rifle into their midst, pausing briefly only to reload, but they were getting closer and closer. The first grappling hook landed on the balcony railing with a metallic cry. A French army hat appeared behind it. He then realised that he had forgotten to quiet himself, his lips rapidly firing poof-poof-poof-poof and his weapon bouncing up and down in his hands. His shirt was soaked with sweat.

The child turned around. For a moment it seemed as if Mother and Grandma were dancing the polka.

Oh no, oh no! The Armies were coming! The fear grabbed his throat: what would the Armies do with poor defenceless Mother and Grandma? He was the only man around with a weapon, a mission, a duty!

Suddenly, he did something that would bring great shame to him later that night.

He transformed the rifle in his hands into a machine gun.

In the morning, the child prepared breakfast for himself and Grandma. He felt like a cheater. Until now, he had fended off the attacking Armies only with weapons that belonged to their own period. This was the first time he had cheated. But there were so many of them! Never before had they come in such numbers and so fearlessly. He was the last line of defence, and should he fail, his poor Mother and Grandma would be at the mercy of the Armies.

Now at the kitchen table, he became aware of his movements. It felt as if the handle of the knife with which he cut the ham had just called out to him. Yes, he needed more weapons. He searched the cupboard and later, when Grandma went to the bathroom, he hid the biggest knife under his mattress.

The weekend approached and Brigitte still hadn't returned the man. Since it was almost Sunday, Mother was careful not to hit Grandma in the face or across her hands, but Grandma showed no such restraint: she tried to scratch her daughter's face. Hence the fights were slower and more cautious, though just as forceful.

The Armies sensed victory. The child no longer thought twice about his weapons; he even went as far as deploying nuclear bombs. The Armies, however, also ceased to obey the rules of their respective time periods, Neanderthals charging into battle side by side with futuristic aliens. They were already climbing onto the balcony, the glass resonating under their axes, forcing the child to use laser beams to cut down the first waves. This time, the corpses did not simply fall down. They also bled. More and more of them gushed bloody geysers as their limbs were ripped off. These sights mingled with the screams of the wounded who were trampled by the next waves of attackers.

Reinforcements were coming. The child had strung a thin steel rope between the apartment buildings, and now they fell into the trap. Heads rolled off vehicles and landed with a dull sound on the bloody ground.

In the evening, the child was so tired he could barely move. He couldn't sleep at night anymore, and he no longer listened to Grandma's breathing, preferring to look out of the window instead. He felt the gaze of the Armies upon him. They were out there in the dark, in the morning watching him on his way to school. It was there, in that strange world where girls chattered about things they had bought the previous day and where boys pinched the girls, that the Armies did not exist. But their absence did not bring the child relief. Only ceaseless worry about what they would do to Mother and Grandma when they returned. During class, he could suddenly see his family's bloodied, butchered corpses, barely recognisable from the shreds of their clothes. He groaned in horror, so loud that the teacher sent him home. He seemed ill anyway, she said. Let him get better over the weekend.

As he walked home, the child kept stopping. He'd prefer to go elsewhere, somewhere there were no Armies. But then Mother and Grandma wouldn't be safe!

Grandma was sleeping as he crumbled into his corner.

He looked out of the window. Several mothers were strolling across the courtyard with baby carriages, comparing their children as if they were prizes that they had won.

If only Brigitte would return that man!

He was tired from all the evil that was out there. The courtyard seemed ordinary and casual. None of the people in those apartments could sense the evil that marched in their midst. An evil that wanted to get to Mother and Grandma. Even the two of them weren't aware of it. It was his secret, his alone. His only responsibility.

At first he noticed white specks floating across his vision, then he saw that they were gathering around the borders of his view, trimming the courtyard in white. The specks spread like cotton in the breeze, covering everything. He sank into the white oblivion, the horizon disappearing and the apartment buildings with it.

The only thing he could say, so as to prove his own existence, was: 'I'm alone.'

He imagined an astronaut from the movies drifting into milky space. He was moving, but his efforts were in vain. He grabbed for something with his hands, but there was nothing there. He breathed, but his supply of air was limited. His heart was beating, but there was no point.

The child squeezed his eyelids hard, his tears stopped, and he waited, afraid to open his eyes to the white again.

'I have to do my duty,' he said, and looked.

He saw Mother walking across the courtyard. Her furious steps told him that Brigitte hadn't returned the man. The child looked at Grandma. Her mouth hung open, and she was snoring loudly. He thought about waking her, telling her to prepare for the battle.

Mother's footsteps stopped in front of the door.

He had to save both of them!

He grabbed the baseboard with his right hand, and with his left, slid the knife from under the mattress.

He got up. For the first time ever, he would meet the Armies on his feet.

'Come, Armies,' he said boldly. 'Give me the chance to fight for hope and glory!'

When the loud cries of the final battle had ceased, a neighbour called the police. They came and knocked heavily on the door a couple of times, and the door opened. The policeman who entered first thought that the helplessly weeping child in the corner had spilt chocolate sauce all over himself.

There are those who say that there's evil done every minute in the City of London, but they haven't seen anything until they walk through the doors of the Grasshopper Escapement, and find out what's counting down those minutes...

The Time of Your Life

Lucinda Bromfield

My trembling fingers hover over the watch, just above the worn leather strap. I don't dare to touch it. I don't know what will happen if I do. It's one of the first ever split-second chronographs, with elegant, sprawling black numbers lazing on a white enamel face. Twenty-six years ago my father dangled it over my cot. Ninety years ago, in 1922, my great grandfather bought it to celebrate starting our firm. I stare, mesmerised by the magical way the four sculpted hands, two thick and two thin, chase each other in never-ending circles.

My future used to be as smooth and certain as those watch hands. I would qualify as a solicitor with the family firm. When my father retired, the watch would be presented to me as I took my place as managing partner. I remember the anticipation that bubbled through me, daydreaming about my glorious expectations while I waited for my father to finish work for the day. In his dim office the watch shone, capturing all the light in the room and swallowing it whole.

'See Matthew,' he'd say, tapping its face, 'time is of the essence. That's what we put in the contracts for perishables, for building projects, for business ventures. This…' he'd fling his arms wide to encompass all the dusty streets of legal London, from the Royal Courts of Justice to Lincoln's Inn Fields, 'is nothing without time; it runs on time from the billable hour to the split-second reprieve.' He would thrust the watch at me, pointing to the two thin hands as they counted away the seconds.

'Time is all we have, Matthew. Have you used yours wisely today?'

There will be no grand presentation. My father died six months ago and my faith in reality is gone. Not all at once, not in the shock of cold in the morgue or in the stillness of the house without him. My faith dripped away second by second as, with inexorable slowness, I lost the belief that the world is rational and safe.

Perhaps I could have been saved had I allowed the policemen (the ones who told me about my father's death) to call someone for me. But I have no family and did not want to burden a friend. For two days I stayed away from work and made the necessary phone calls. I think I ate soup from a tin. When I woke on the third day I saw, on my bedside table, the clear plastic bag I'd been given at the morgue. It held Father's wallet, watch, and silk handkerchief, the possessions he'd had on him when he died. It seemed very important to return everything to its accustomed place, so I took the bag and for the first time since his death, entered my father's bedroom. It smelled of him, ivory shaving soap underlined with a hint of coffee and cigars. If I shut my eyes I could pretend he was still there, fussing with his cufflinks.

I found the note crushed into the bottom of the watch case, light coloured against the dark silk lining, dry and fragile under my fingertips, folded upon itself so often that the creases had worn through in places. The paper was warm, almost animal to the touch, like the vellum deeds we keep in the firm's safe. Faded black writing crawled across it, the letter 's' sometimes appearing as 'ʃ', the sort of thing you see in Shakespeare folios or old legal documents. It said:

> 'The undersigned, for themselves and their heirs in trust, agree that all alterations, additions, and fixings of this watch shall be contrived by M. Lucas Esquire of The Grasshopper Escapement, 107 Serle Street, London.'

The signatures were in a darker, rustier ink, too faded to read now, more like stains than names.

As if someone had switched on a light in my brain to illuminate long ago memories, I recalled the Grasshopper Escapement. Waiting with Mr Lucas for my father to return from a meeting and pick up the watch was one of my favourite times; it was incomprehensible that I had forgotten it.

When I went to Mr Lucas' shop as a child I always sat on the same stool, too high for my feet to touch the ground, but sturdy nonetheless. From my stool I could look though the open doorway and watch people speeding by. Lawyers in suits or wig and gown, students in jeans, business people in their smart clothes. Some of them sipped coffee from plain white takeaway cups. The ubiquitous Starbucks didn't exist back then.

Everything in the shop was cosy and clean and light. Any unpleasantness from the outside world faded as it passed the threshold. No petrol fumes or fast food smells. Even the air sparkled, as if it had been polished along with the wooden counter and the glass display cases. The busy atmosphere of the London streets, rich with the heat of summer dust, or frigid with winter drizzle, did not intrude. Whatever the weather, it never seemed to affect the sunny interior of the shop. The Grasshopper Escapement was like an unchanging cocoon, always warm and safe. Mr Lucas would talk to me while we waited.

'See them, Matt? All those little lives, rushing about as if they had all the time in the world, never understanding the value of what they possess, so careless of it that they throw it away with hurry... You won't be like that when you grow up, will you, Matt?'

When I assured him I would not, with the solemnity that only a four-year-old can muster, Mr Lucas would nod, wink one twinkling blue eye and offer me a lollipop from the jar he kept under the counter.

Standing in my dead father's bedroom, the plastic bag dangling from my numb fingers, I never wanted anything as much as I wanted to be back in Mr Lucas' shop, sucking a lollipop, waiting. It was quiet in the bedroom, a sort of waiting silence. I had the strange impression that if I lay down on the bed and drew the heavy covers over me I would cease to exist, that the silence would absorb me. When I went to put the watch back into its case I realised it had stopped. I tried to wind it, but the tiny grooved knob would not turn for me. The watch's silence in the silent house was unbearable; I grabbed my coat and set out.

The Grasshopper Escapement Jewellers has been around since 1720. It said so on the smart green sign, complete with gold writing and a picture of a gold grasshopper, which hung from a pole above the door. The sign ticked like a clock as it swung back and forth in the doorway, so loud that I could hear it despite the street noise. Inside all was quiet and calm. Mr Lucas sat behind the shiny wooden counter, flanked by sparkling glass cases of precious things. He could have stepped straight out of my memory, faded tweed suit tailored to his short, heavy frame, salt-and-pepper hair and whiskers, everything perfect, fixed.

'Matthew!' Mr Lucas smiled across at me, then his face changed, concern creasing his forehead. 'Of course. Your father. I am so sorry.' He said it like he meant it, as if it was a personal sorrow, not like the morgue assistant's perfunctory 'sorry for your loss'.

'Thank you.' I moved to the counter to be nearer his comforting presence. My stool was still there, only now my feet reached the ground. As I sat down, the cool calm of the shop eased through me. I took a long, full breath. It felt like my first since I had seen the policemen standing in the firm's reception area, waiting for me.

I gave Mr Lucas the watch, which he opened with a tiny screwdriver, laying the vulnerable innards bare. Shiny metal cogs sat within cogs, each piece still. He lifted the watch into his hands to replace the back and it whirred into life, making a tiny, clicking tick. I couldn't see what Mr Lucas had done to restart it, but I could see the hands sweeping round again. My pulse gave a joyful skip.

'Thank you,' I said, making to put the watch back into its case. Mr Lucas frowned.

'Aren't you going to wear it?' There was a slight edge to his voice. 'Really Matt, I think it is what your father would have wanted.' I paused. Reassurance washed out from him, catching me in its wake. I wanted to make Mr Lucas happy. I fastened the watch onto my wrist. He smiled.

I slept well that night and better still over the next three months. There was so much to be done, a managing partner to appoint (I had neither the experience nor the gravitas for the role), the funeral to plan, the estate to settle. With so many concerns I did not notice the tiredness that crept up on me, taking a little more of my energy each day. When I began to spend my evenings and weekends resting on the sofa or in bed, I felt no alarm. It's only natural, I thought, with the death and working as hard as I do. I am happy. I enjoy my work. The constant tick of the watch on my wrist reassured me. Everything was fine, until the accident.

One moment I was rushing to court, nipping through the London traffic as usual, the next I lay sprawled on my back with a blur of buildings above me. At the hospital, the doctors congratulated me on my luck. The car that caught my hip threw me onto the pavement, not into the traffic. It's a shame I stuck my hand out to halt my fall, but a broken wrist is nothing compared to what could have happened. The watch didn't even get scratched. It wouldn't fit over the plaster cast so I put it away in its case.

Over the next couple of weeks I started to feel better. With my renewed energy everything seemed easier. I didn't miss the watch. Like most of my colleagues I used my smartphone and computer to tell the time.

This morning, about a month after the accident, Mr Lucas called me at the office.

'Matt?' His voice was hesitant, scratchy. He sounded exhausted. 'Is everything okay?'

'Yes, thanks, apart from a broken wrist.'

'So you aren't wearing the watch? You can wear on your right arm, you know, face on the underside of your wrist, like the Americans.'

'Actually, I'm managing fine with my phone. What can I do for you?'

'Oh, nothing in particular. Now it's just you, I thought I'd give you a call. I was very fond of your father, you know.'

'That's kind of you...'

'You're using your phone, you say? Lots of people do now.' He sighed. 'Will you wear the watch again, do you think?'

'Oh yes.' I wanted to reassure him, to repay him for thinking of me. 'Of course.'

That odd conversation has been looping through my mind all day. I understand that my thoughts aren't rational, but I can't chase them away. I think about the dragging lethargy that affected me while I wore the watch. I know how much better I feel without it on my wrist.

Which is why I'm standing here, in my dead father's room, more afraid than I have ever been. The horrible trembling moves from my fingers, to my arms, to possess my whole body. I snatch my hand away; this is ludicrous! I'll be fine after a good night's sleep. But I can't sleep. The watch calls to me like a phantom limb. When the day is light enough to make me feel safe, I use kitchen tongs to shut the watch into its case. I take it to the Grasshopper Escapement.

Mr Lucas is still behind the counter, dwarfed by glass cases on either side. The glass still sparkles, but now the jewels on display look tawdry rather than precious. There are shadows in the room, a dimness around its edges. A strange smell hovers in the once clean air; an odd, uncomfortable scent, almost too faint to catch. Mr Lucas no longer looks how I remember him. His tweed suit is worn and patched. His hair is dishevelled; ragged clumps of whiskers fringe his chapped lips.

'Mr Lucas…' I'm not sure what to say. What I am doing is crazy. But I'm going to do it anyway. I put the watch case on the counter. He rests a rheumatic hand on it, knuckles grotesquely swollen.

'Your father understood, Matt. He felt he was the last of a dying breed, like me. Things have changed so much, computers and smartphones, the time from all over the world at your fingertips. I hoped you might share some of your time with me, Matt, in memory of your father. Your watch is the last one, you see.'

I don't reply. As I leave the shop I can feel his faded eyes on me, heavy as years.

I still miss my father. Mostly it is a gentle pressure, a touch so light I can almost forget it. Sometimes it is a detached, frozen feeling as though his death disconnected me from my own life. On these occasions the world seems wrong, imperfect. My counsellor says that this sense of dislocation, of wrongness, will fade in time. I told him about Mr Lucas and the watch. He didn't laugh, or tell me I'm crazy. He just said:

'Grief does funny things to people.'

I suppose he's right. I don't know what happened to Mr Lucas or to the watch.

Perhaps he sold it and made enough to retire. Still, when I go to the Royal Courts of Justice I always hurry past the place where the Grasshopper Escapement used to be. It's a bookshop now, shiny new titles making a blur of colours behind the window. The sign still hangs above the doorway. If you listen hard, you can hear it tick as it swings back and forth, counting away your life one second at a time.

With a friendship filled with misunderstanding, and an almost Gilliamesque yearning for fantasy, there's something about Melanie Whipman's first Fiction Desk story that perfectly captures a certain type of adolescence.

End of the Rope

Melanie Whipman

I've got a good feeling about Ruby. The chair next to mine is pulled out slightly, angled to suggest a welcome. The spare locker's been emptied and sprayed with the honey and vanilla polish I brought from home. I've nicked pencils from the store cupboard, sharpened them to the perfect point that will scribe fine lines but won't snap on an over-firm full stop. Every time the door opens I look up, with a half smile, welcoming but not stalker-eager. But she doesn't come.

Miss Walker called me in yesterday. 'Bridget, dear,' she says, pseudo-solicitous, like she cares. 'We've got a new girl arriving, Ruby Pitcher, and I'd like you to be her buddy.'

It's a funny word, 'buddy.' We had a 'buddying system' in junior school, for any new arrivals, but I get the impression that Miss Walker says it without the apostrophes. Buddy, as in loyal friend. American Army. Does she think it's hip? Cool? I'm so busy thinking about the word and it's uncool connotations that I don't hear the rest of what she says, and when I notice the silence and I look at her, she's got her head on one side, and her eyebrows raised. 'So will you, dear?'

Will I what? 'Sure,' I say.

She arrives when I've given up, just as the lunch bell rings, so when I hear the door open I presume it's some over-eager classmate running out to be first in the queue for Friday's fish and chips, and I miss her entrance. It's Miss Warbuck who has to greet her, and the rest of the class have all got an eyeful while I've still got my head stuck in my desk. When I finally clock her she's everything and more than I could have wanted. I know she'll be my friend. She'll have to be, because the rest of the class sure as hell won't want her. I stand up. 'Sit here,' I say, but my voice and action are lost in the scraping of chairs and the mass exodus of the rest of the class. They push past her in a jostling navy stream and I think she'll be swallowed up and carried away, but when they're all gone she's still standing there, like a princess, a scarlet queen.

'You're not wearing a uniform.'

She tosses back a crimson plait, smoothes her scarlet skirt, folds her arms across her postbox chest. 'Uniforms violate our right to free expression, don't you think?'

That's when I know we're going to be friends.

I keep her close to me all week. She's spiky and funny, and at the weekend we hang out in town. She invites me back to her place. Her bedroom's cooler than mine, full of funky retro stuff in bright pinks and oranges, it's like she's gone out and bought the entire Habitat showroom. The walls are bare though, apart from one weird, dark lumpy painting of a distorted city up in the clouds with a rope dangling down and a tiny figure at the bottom, looking up.

'What d'you think?' she says. 'D'you reckon that's me, in the picture?'

Sure enough, when I look closely it does look a bit like her. The same red hair and even those dungarees she's got on now.

'At night I disappear,' she says, 'dissolve right through the paint. I go up into the clouds, there's a whole city up there. You just need a drop of blood. Just a thumb prick.'

'Yeah, right.' I go over to her old record player. 'Vinyls. Cool. Can I put some on?'

'Look.' She pulls back her sleeve. 'Promise not to tell.'

There's a tattoo ladder up her forearm. White scar slashes at the bottom, then the rungs getting redder and rawer, and at the top they're all crusty and oozing.

My stomach swirls. 'Why d'you do it?'

'To get into the picture,' she says. 'Do you want to see?'

And I'm wondering what I'm supposed to say, whether this is some kind of weird joke, and then her dad comes in, and I'm saved from saying something stupid. He's your normal kind of dad, shapeless in that thin-but-fat way, styleless brown hair that's been 'trimmed' for a hundred years, tan slippers, and clothes from another decade.

'Can't you knock?' She turns to me, her sleeves pulled down, and gives me a look that's supposed to mean something. I feel a bit sorry for her dad because he's got a mug in each hand and a pack of Bourbons tucked under his left arm and Ruby's acting all arsy.

'I'll get it,' I say and I'm trying to take the biscuits and one of the mugs, and he's laughing and taking the mug back because it's too hot to hold without the handle, and then he's putting them on Ruby's shiny kidney-shaped dressing table and coming back and taking my hand and checking it's not burnt, which is a bit of an overkill but quite sweet. And all the time Ruby's acting like a stroppy mare, saying nothing and staring at the carpet.

'Thanks,' I say. 'Just what we need, a cup of tea.'

'Where's Mum?'

'Sleeping.' He reaches out and strokes her hair, bunching it up in both hands. 'She's tired. She's on nights this week. Tell you what, if you're still here at six I'll bring you both a beer. D'you girls drink beer, or is it all that sweet pop stuff these days. What is it? Bacardi Breezes?'

'Breezers.' I'm laughing too, but feeling kind of squishy inside because I haven't seen my dad for such a long time now, and we used to be like this once, a proper family.

Ruby's got her arms folded. 'She's not staying. We've got homework.'

'Anything I can help with? Vocab test?'

'She's got to go, Dad.'

'She's right, I better go.' I'm not staying where I'm not wanted. 'Bye Ruby, see you tomorrow, and thanks very much,' I say, and he smiles and touches my shoulder in apology as I walk past. And I wish I had a dad like him.

I get home and Mum's at the sewing machine again, making pillow cases or cushion covers or something.

'Your dad phoned.' She raises her voice above the burr of the machine, her eyes on her fingertips and the jerking needle. 'He wants to see you.'

'I don't want to talk to him.' In the old days I would have told her about how weird Ruby is and the self-harming thing, and how friendly her dad is, but now she never seems to listen.

She takes her foot off the pedal and looks at me. 'You ought to see him,' she says, even though he's divorced her and buggered off and just left us both. Then my phone buzzes. It's Ruby: a smiley face and a *soz, buy u hot choc 2morro*.

I figure self-harming's not so bad. There's girls in my school who vomit out their lunch in the loo, some who are so skinny you can see through them, there's glue-sniffers behind the science block with their heads stuffed in Spar bags, and skiving coke addicts who hang around outside the school and try and sell you stuff. So on that scale, Ruby's pretty normal. I send back a smiley face.

She skips Games four weeks running. I warn her Mrs Carder's got a calendar and a log book, but she says it all the same, her head on one side, fingers twisting a lock of red hair. 'I can't do PE today, Mrs Carder, I've got my period.'

Mrs Carder is a lesbo-rhinocerous. Helmet-hair, skin tough as hide, head pushed forward on a lumpy neck. She gets her diary out, shoves through the pages with a fat thumb. 'Not today, Ruby. Can't be today, another two weeks. And if you're irregular, that's a shame, but that's what sanitary pads are for. Have you seen the advertisements, girls in skimpy shorts doing all sorts?'

Ruby's kitted out from lost property. We're in the gym but I've given her my tracksuit top to cover her arms.

It's rope climbing. She stands there next to the rope, just pushing it so it sways, and Mrs Carder's saying, 'Up you get then girls, no time like the present, cheer up, these aren't hangman ropes. Take that top off, Ruby. You need bare arms to grip with.'

And I look at Ruby to see how she's taking it, only she's vanished, there's just the swinging rope and I look up and she's right at the top, hanging upside down.

I feel warm inside.

And Mrs Carder loves her, despite her wild red hair and her fake period. Where d'you learn to do that, we ask, and Ruby's grinning, saying you never know when you need to escape. And

Carder's nodding and snorting and saying it was an Olympic sport once and it's all about strength and courage and speed. 'Do it again,' she says.

The whole class is staring. She's so smooth, it's like watching coke come up a straw. Legs wrapped round, feet gripping, hands at nose level, feet loose, knees up, feet hugging the rope again, hands shifting up, knees up, feet pinching again and again. Tight and deft. She looks safe up there.

She invites me home, makes me tea. 'Don't worry, Dad's out.'

I shrug. 'I like him. He's nice. And he's here, not like my dad.'

Outside a car engine revs and there's a snatch of laughter. She squeezes the teabags between two spoons and drops them in the sink.

'I mean it, you're so lucky,' I say. 'My dad's buggered off with some woman from work. I mean, what a cliché. He can't even be original. And Mum's forgiven him. Expects me to go and hang out with him, like it's all normal.'

'I wish my dad would bugger off.'

I think how pathetic and ungrateful she is. 'Jesus, Ruby, you're clueless.'

She thumps the cups down on the side so hard the tea slops over, 'Bridget, you don't know...' and I'm about to walk out and she grabs my hand, 'Come on, forget it.'

We go upstairs and she sits on her desk, and looks over at the painting. I hitch myself up next to her and look at it too. It kind of pulls you in.

'How come you're so good on the rope?'

'Practice.' She unfolds a paperclip and starts cleaning her nails. 'You never know when you'll need it.'

'So when's your dad back?'

'Soon. Mum's on shifts tonight. He'll be here when she's gone. Bridget, what's your dad like? Why don't you want to see him? Has he done something?'

'Yes! He's left us. Buggered off.'

She reaches down and pulls open a drawer, 'We're best friends aren't we?'

'Sure.'

And next thing I know she's got out a razor blade, and is yanking up her sleeve, and it's against her arm, forty-five degrees, and she does it in one slash. The split in her skin is pale for a second before the blood comes seeping up, like it's planning its entrance, a little hesitation to build the tension. And I don't think to stop her. We look at it, the two of us, like her arm's some kind of spectacle, which I guess it is.

'Promise not to tell.' And then she's smearing in a finger, running it along the line of the cut like she's checking out a seam, like Miss Symonds in needlework. And then she's walking over to the painting on the wall. 'The school jumble sale, at my last school,' she says, 'that's where the painting came from. I knew as soon as I saw it that it was supposed to be me.'

And she's got her hand held out in front of her, finger pad up, like she's balancing a contact lens or something. And then she's kneeling on her bed, face to face with the picture, pressing her fingertip against the red dungarees of the painted figure.

She's freaking me out. I'm thinking of the *Little Shop of Horrors*. Feed me! Feed me! And I half expect the kid in the picture to reach out a canvas arm and drag Ruby in. Course nothing happens. Ruby sort of sighs and lies back on the bed, on her funky Habitat duvet, sucking at her arm, eyes closed.

'Don't you ever just want to escape?' she says.

I don't know if she's trying to mess with me and this is her twisted sense of humour. Or whether it's for real. Either way it isn't normal, and I leave her to it.

Mum's at the door when I get home, all shiny and smiley. 'Your dad's going to take you out for a pizza. He's coming at seven.'

'I can't. I'm out already.'

I go down to the park and hang around on the swings, remembering how Dad used to push me so high it felt like I was flying. My phone keeps buzzing but I ignore it. On the way home I see Ruby's dad, coming out of the Dog and Pheasant. He's all over the place, so drunk he doesn't even see me.

Ruby has a burn on her face at school the next day. She slept against the radiator. I take her to the school nurse and she says it happens if you're a heavy sleeper, she's seen that kind of thing before in A&E.

But Ruby's radiator's under the window, opposite the bed. I picture her holding a kettle against her face. 'You ought to see someone.' I tell her. She just looks at me and shakes her head.

Her dad's waiting outside the school when we finish. 'Hey. Thought we could go shopping. Hi Bridget, how you doing?'

'Good thanks.'

He's got that grey hung-over look.

'So, did your parents name you after Bardot? You look a bit like her, you know?'

I shrug and avoid Ruby's eyes.

'Hey, come with us,' he squeezes my shoulder and flicks my hair, 'if you fancy it. I'm treating Ruby, buying her a new phone. Could grab a coffee, hot chocolate.'

I mumble something about homework.

On Monday I'm buddy-less, she's not at school.

We hear about it on Tuesday. Three policemen come in. They ask for me. I get to sit in the headmaster's office, and the policeman offers me his plate of custard creams. They ask a million questions. No boyfriends, I say, no internet dating, no drugs, no strange behaviour. I don't mention the razor blade.

Mum and I watch her parents on the news that night. Her mother is little and blonde, she tugs at her lips with bitten nails. Her dad looks smaller; his appeal is slow and shaky, and his eyes are all skitty.

Different newspapers say different things. Someone saw a redhead at the coach station. Ruby's Dad is helping them with their enquiries. They've confiscated his computers.

I go round there after school. It's that soft, misty rain that makes everything unfocussed and grey. Ruby would have hated it. The gate creaks, and upstairs there's movement behind her window. I get to the door, my finger on the bell, but I can't do it. I'm walking away when the door opens. 'Bridget? Is that you, love?'

He comes down the path, his slippers sloshing in the puddles.

'Come in Bridget, come in.' He gives me a hug, his hand rubbing the small of my back. His breath's all beery. 'I'm glad you're here.' He takes my arm, pulls me in. 'What can I get you? Beer? Glass of wine?'

'Can I see her room?'

It hasn't changed. Her nightdress is still sticking out from the side of her pillow, there's a bent paperclip on the desk. The painting is where it always was, the clouds are brighter than I remember, as if the sun's about to set, or maybe rise. I go closer, pressing my knees against the bed. It's changed. Or maybe I've just remembered it wrong. The girl's at the top of the rope, one hand reaching for the clouds.

'She was obsessed with that picture.' He's right behind me, so close I can hear the suck and click of his throat as he gulps down his wine. 'I bought it for her. I liked buying her presents.'

He looks at the picture over my head, his hand gripping my shoulder. 'Never understood why she liked it.'

My heart's thumping against the base of my throat.

'Did she ever talk about me?' His breath's hot and huffy against my ear. 'What did she say? Have you heard from her?'

My phone buzzes. I fish it one-handed from my pocket. 'Dad.' My stomach's swirling and clenching. 'Can you come and get me?'

'They think I've done something to her. I never hurt her.' His jaw's clenched and he's sucking in air through his teeth. 'I know what they're saying. But I didn't fucking hurt her.'

'I've got to go.' I back away from him, holding up my hand. Behind him, in the picture, Ruby's hand is touching the clouds.

Searchers after horror haunt strange, far places, as a man once said. For them are the catacombs of Ptolemais, and the carven mausolea of the nightmare countries... they might also want to check out a certain biker bar on the North Circular. Just ask Bernie Deehan.

Hell for Leather

Bernie Deehan

I hate the sound of breaking glass. Always have. When I worked in pubs, if I ever dropped a stack of empties on my way back to the bar, I'd always get a big cheer from the room. Why do people do that? I'll tell you why: because it happened to someone else. It's funny if it's not you.

Sometimes though, you might wish it were you that had the bad luck. You might wish it with your whole heart. I ought to know.

Let me explain what I mean. By the mid-nineties I'd pulled myself together, moved back to London and got a job installing burglar alarms. Good gig, steady money, bit of cash-in-hand stuff on the side.

One day my pager went off in the van. I rang the office from a phone box, light rain tapping at the panes. It was Lynn: would I go to some place near Wembley, needs a full alarm system, the works, by tonight.

'Tonight? I'm not Paul Daniels.'

She stressed the urgency, how everyone else was tied up. And then she told me how much of a bonus I'd get.

'Tonight? No problem. What's the address?'

'Place called the Jet Cafe, on the North Circular. Heard of it?'

The rain pressed heavier on the glass.

'Terry...? Terry?'

'That place closed down years ago.'

'The guy told me it's about to reopen.'

I couldn't believe it. 'I can't do the job,' I said. 'Sorry, I just can't.'

Lynn pleaded with me. We had a thing going, me and Lynn, which had surprised both of us. We weren't exactly in the flush of youth. I liked her a lot.

'Please, Terry. If we don't do it now, they'll find someone who will. It's a big contract.'

I could see a possible future with Lynn. Some quiet suburb, a little garden, finally some peace. I didn't want to mess things up.

'Terry?'

'Okay, okay. I'll do it.'

I hung up. The Jet Cafe. Those three words together formed an unpleasant circuit in my stomach. I'd wiped the place from my mind, or at least tried to during my waking hours, but now here it was, steaming back like a ten-ton truck.

I thought about calling back, telling her I'd changed my mind, but money was money. And Lynn was Lynn. I'd lost too much time I had to make up for. I climbed in the van and got going.

Let me tell you about the Jet Cafe. It sits on the North Circular, a road that does exactly what it says: it spans the top half of London before joining up with the South Circular.

Together they form a traffic-heavy band of tarmac right around the capital. I covered the South London jobs, so had managed to avoid the North Circular so far – and I'd intended to keep it that way.

In the late thirties, a roadside caff opened up. It did its job well, keeping motorists fed and watered. By the late fifties the Jet Cafe had become a beacon for bikers in black leather. It had a fearsome reputation – the tables and chairs were bolted to the floor – but it held an irresistible pull for petrolheads. The smell of motor oil, bacon sarnies washed down with strong tea, rock 'n' roll on the jukebox... it was heaven.

I started going there in the early sixties, pulling in on my battered Triumph Thunderbird, always a good half-minute before Colin on his Norton Manx. I always beat him on the road.

We'd met in junior school. I saved him from the school bully, administering a broken nose to Tony Broadstairs outside the science block. Colin had looked up to me from then on, poor bugger. We discovered a common interest in motorbikes, as in riding imaginary ones round the perimeter of the school playground. I always won of course, having longer legs. He was like the brother I never had.

After school we got boring jobs in factories and scraped the money together to turn our imaginary bikes into real ones; both second-hand of course, and in need of constant attention, but our pride and joy nevertheless.

We were knocking around, hanging out at the Jet Cafe, trying to avoid turning into our dads. The bikes gave us an identity, freedom, the possibility of a bit of skirt.

What happened next... it was about a girl. It's always about a girl.

The North Circular's been rebuilt since those days – more lanes, much more traffic – but as I approached Wembley in the van it felt just the same. Up ahead, I could make out the large white building on the left through the rain-sloshed windscreen. The moisture left my mouth.

I slowed down, then considered speeding the hell away. The driver behind me hit his horn twice. I flicked on the left indicator and pulled off the North Circular, trying to regulate my breathing. The Jet Cafe sign was different, the big neon letters gone, but the building looked exactly the same. And my God, that forecourt. It could have told some stories.

The place didn't look much different inside. It was astonishing, like I'd just stepped back thirty-five years. The new owner, Mark, told me what he wanted.

'I thought this place was gone,' I said. I'd hoped.

'It was. Became a tyre place for years. I put on a reunion here a few years ago. Packed out it was, everyone wanted it back. Scraped some money together and here we are.'

He swept his hand round the room with pride. They were opening the next day, big ceremony planned, blues and skiffle bands and all sorts.

'You remember this place?' he said.

'Me? No,' I said. 'Never been here.'

I took my gear out of the van and got cracking. Do the job, speed off back to South London. End of. I started with some sensors above the doors, but couldn't stop staring out of the large windows. Force of habit. Many's the rainy evening when I'd look out, nursing a mug of tea gone cold, waiting for the headlights of a red Mini to flash across the wet glass. Carol. I'd cried myself to sleep over her many a night, but I'd act nonchalant in the Jet Cafe, as young men do. So would Colin, sitting there in his leathers, looking at the table, blowing bubbles into his Coke bottle with a straw.

Everyone wanted Carol and didn't she know it.

'All right, Carol!'

'Oi, lovely legs!'

'Gizza twirl, sweetheart!'

She walked this gauntlet like a movie star, a world away from her day job behind the counter at Woolies.

I played the long game, the pretending-not-to-see-her game. I don't know why I thought that would work. But that night she came up and sat right down next to us. Colin's Coke bubbled furiously.

'Here, how comes you never say anything when I come in?' she said to me.

'Cos you're a lady,' I said, surprising myself.

'Buy us a Coke then, loverboy.' She winked and my heart imploded.

I went up to the counter like a lap dog. I knew Colin wouldn't say anything to her: he was far too shy. But when I came back to the table I found her stroking his hair, and this carried on once I'd sat down. He was talking away to her too, the sly devil, saying more than he ever did to me, and she was eating it up.

'Don't listen to him,' I said.

'Why, what have you got to say for yourself?' said Carol.

Good question. 'I let my bike do the talking.'

'Oh yeah? Colin was just telling me about his bike, how he could beat you easy.'

'I didn't say that,' said Colin.

'Oh, really?' I said.

'I really didn't –'

'How about the Chicken Run then?' I said. 'For the hand of this fair maiden.' I didn't know where the words were coming from, but I liked the sound of them.

Colin looked scared.

The Chicken Run was a Jet Cafe thing. The riders would mount up, someone put a song on the jukebox, and they'd have to race down to a specified spot on the North Circular, turn around and be back in the caff before the song ended. Winner takes all. It was lethal. But I'd beat Colin easy, no question, and Carol would be mine.

Such is the wisdom of the young.

'Yeah, the Chicken Run!' said Carol. 'Hey everyone! We got a Chicken Run!'

'No, hang on –' said Colin.

'Chicken Run! Chicken Run!'

'Chicken Run!'

'Chicken Run! Yeaahhhh!'

The deafening sound of forks and mugs bashing on the tables. Colin shook his head at me. He looked like a little boy.

Carol turned those big brown eyes my way: well, loverboy?

'Saddle up, Col.'

'No, Terry...'

The whole place was chanting now, even the waitresses. We had no choice. I grabbed Colin's arm and forced him out of his seat. Carol squeezed my arm. 'My hero,' she said.

We walked to the doors, Colin squirming in my grasp. I pointed to the jukebox.

'Gene Vincent, *Race With The Devil*.'

'Come on, Terry. A joke's a joke,' said Colin.

'Relax,' I whispered. 'Just take it slow, let me win, like you always do.' I ruffled his hair; he always hated that.

Carol came out, gave us both a kiss on the cheek. Colin seemed emboldened by it.

'Just take it easy, all right?' I said into his ear.

He pushed me away. I suddenly felt protective, scared for myself as well, but it was too late to back out now. I'd never have any chance with Carol if I called it off.

'Down to the Shell garage and back,' I said. I revved up, Colin revved harder. I looked at Carol: she gazed at Colin first, for longer than I'd liked, before turning her eyes to me. Everything was at stake.

Throttles were twisted, burning up the forecourt, a waitress held a red tea towel above her head, waited for the needle to drop on Gene Vincent... the towel whipped down and we were off.

We banked onto the road, not even looking for oncoming traffic. Soon the wind was whipping into my face. I looked back and Colin was too close for comfort. Faster, faster... zigzagging through the traffic and the beeps from irate drivers in their modest little motors.

We were at the Shell garage in a flash, Colin at my heels. 'Slow down, Col!' I shouted. Then I signalled to let him know I was mounting the traffic island to cross to the opposite side. But when I looked behind he'd beaten me to it and was already on his way back.

I cleared the island and slapped on the speed. I couldn't believe he was ahead, I just couldn't believe it. He looked back, gave me the finger. Then I saw the truck ahead of him braking fast, way too fast, but he was still looking back at me and laughing.

'Colin! The truck! COLIN!'

You can guess the rest.

I didn't stay for the funeral. I fled to Southend like the coward I am, an exile in a seaside town. I left everything: my parents, my job, my friends. They never forgave me. I got bar work, shifts as a nightwatchman, club bouncer, the odd bit of bailiff stuff for a local loan shark, no questions asked, nothing too heavy. I did it all. I never rode a motorbike again. Days bled into weeks, into months, years, all marinated in Guinness and whisky. It wasn't much of a life. Sometimes I wondered why I bothered.

On the nights I wasn't working, I'd lie awake staring at the pulse of headlights through the thin curtains, not wanting to succumb to sleep and all that waited there. Sleep was a TV with only one channel and only one thing ever played: the sound of shattering glass, the shards showering the tarmac like black rain, the dull thud of a body against a metal door, a head snapped back, bones splintering, a young man turned into a spineless rag doll in black leather pulled backwards through the air.

I often wondered what he would have done with his life; surely more than I had. Every wasted day was a slap in his face, every tumbler of Johnnie Walker a splash on his grave. Not that I'd ever seen his grave.

And now here I was, back in the Jet Cafe. Full circle.

'How's it going?' said Mark from the bottom of the ladder.

'What? Oh, fine. I've got the front section done.'

'Look,' he said, 'the staff have gone home to get some beauty sleep. Big day tomorrow. Can I leave you to it? I trust you not to nick anything. Just call me with the code before the morning. Okay?'

I felt uneasy. 'Okay, no problem.'

I watched him drive off, leaving the forecourt empty. I looked around the lonely room. There was a pristine jukebox in the corner, almost exactly where the original used to stand. I needed a drink, something to calm the nerves. There were beers in the fridges behind the counter; they wouldn't miss a couple of bottles. The first one felt good, the cold lager flowing through my insides, steadying the ship. The second was even more reassuring, as was the third, the fourth.

Three hours later, I was flat out on one of the long benches that ran the length of the tables. I woke with a start. A song was blasting out from somewhere, a tune that sent a chill through me. Gene Vincent, *Race With The Devil*. I sat up on the bench, rubbed my aching head. The song was coming from the jukebox, which pulsed with life, glowing red and yellow in the semi-darkness.

Had I turned the jukebox on before I passed out? Unlikely: I wouldn't have gone anywhere near it.

'Hello?' I said.

The jukebox cut off. I stayed on the bench, afraid to move. I don't know how long I sat there. At some point I decided enough was enough and stood up, walked slowly to the jukebox. The plug was lying loose on the floor, the wall socket empty.

Then I heard the sound of an engine, outside on the forecourt. Sounded an awful lot like a Norton Manx. Colin's bike. It's just the wind and the rain, I reasoned, walking slowly towards the windows. It was lashing down outside but there was definitely an engine revving, getting louder. Goading.

'Colin?' The sound of his name in my mouth made me well up, such a long time since I'd said it. It wasn't him, it couldn't be. Too much drink, that's all.

The jukebox came on again, the one that wasn't plugged in. Still Gene Vincent, mid-song. I opened the glass door and walked outside into the wet night. There was nothing there, nothing at all, but the engine noise was deafening, the sound of burning rubber on concrete. He was here.

'Colin! I know it's you! I'm sorry, Col! I'm so sorry!'

The engine sound moved away from me, towards the lip of the road and then onto the North Circular. I ran after it, warm tears mixing with the rain.

'Colin, wait! Please!'

I ran into the road after him, feeling a sudden lightness, the weight of years falling off my shoulders, running, running, cars honking, I'd catch up with him, I'd catch up, following the sound of the Norton as it weaved in and out of the traffic.

I felt the rush of the car behind me before it hit, before it slammed into my back, the windscreen cracking, and then the blackness...

It's a lot easier now, existence. More streamlined. I still hate the sound of breaking glass, but it doesn't bring that feeling of guilt anymore, the guilt of the living. I race the North Circular, the South Circular, the eternal ringroad, always chasing Colin, round and round we go, round and round.

We race. And he always wins.

If there's one thing that the 2013 horsemeat scandal proved, it's that we never quite know what's in our food. It could be anything... or anyone. Now, who's for cake?

Twice a Day with Water

Die Booth

When Bren sees the cake, it's like it just appeared there, even though he knows logically that it's probably been sitting there on the kitchen table for hours, or even days, and he's just not noticed it before. If he works it out, then it's most likely been there for, what – he checks the clock, 9:15am – about nine hours since Lyndsey left. He can't be entirely sure he didn't put it there himself and then forget, but then he doesn't know why he'd have something like that in the house in the first place.

The cake is pink.

The cake is a lurid, waxy shade of pink, slightly dulled in places with a powdery white sheen. It looks somehow brighter than the rest of the kitchenette, as if the colour in the room has been turned down in comparison, like one of those arty black and white photos of women with red lips that you see on blank greetings cards. Bren pulls out the kitchen chair with a honking scrape of lino and sits with his elbows on the table. One pink fondant fancy, set in the middle of a glass plate. He puts out one hand and picks the cake up: it's harder than he'd expected, the icing stale, and when he turns it over, the pale yellow sponge underneath is dry as the foam tennis balls he used to feed to the dog when he was little. He picks at a piece of the white-streaked pink and it snaps off in a shard. Placing his fingertip against the hard lump on the top of the cake, he presses a fingernail in and feels the icing give way, collapsing into the still-soft cream beneath with the feeling of something dying. Then he puts the cake into the bin and the plate into the sink.

When Bren coughs, his chest twangs with it and he brings up something hard and gelatinous and blood-tasting. It seems disgusting to spit – even though he's alone, he has the odd anxiety of being watched – so he swallows it again and gags. The view from the window is always the same: grey strip of road, grey pavement, and the thin, grey rule of the ocean wall. The sea is in, grey water covering the shivering beach, and the grey sky washes into the waves, the horizon invisible between horizontal colourless layers all the shades of a 1960s television spectrum. It reminds him of his day-to-day life.

Life isn't always like that, though.

The next time Lyndsey visits, she brings along a bottle of vodka, one up from supermarket brand with a Russian name picked out in Cyrillic letters, in peeling gold foil on red. Bren won't have his fix when anyone else is there. It's a private pleasure which needs no distractions for best effect. So they get drunk instead, even though alcohol tastes like bleach to him now, and they watch TV and talk. But the next day, when Lyndsey has gone home and Bren notices the shot glass of clear liquid on the kitchen table, he remembers the previous night and he knows where it must have come from.

Drink me.

Something about that little glass, sitting innocently on the gingham pattern Formica tabletop makes Bren think of the pink cake. Bren doesn't really eat much; his appetite isn't what it used to be and nor is his bank balance. He buys twelve-pence loaves of doughy, white bread and eats slices with chilli sauce spread on them, to give them some kind of discernable taste. In the thin light of morning with his guts echoing, Bren rolls the glass around between his fingers and the liquid inside looks viscous as a lava lamp, as if forming secret messages or teeming with microscopic life. Bren thinks he meant to pour it down the sink, but he absentmindedly drinks it instead.

It's a perfect day for it. Not for a drink, in particular, but for some well-deserved downtime. Tasting that singular smell in the back of his throat, he waits for the euphoria he knows won't come. He washes the shot glass in the sink and clears his works away and wipes down the kitchen table. His head starts to pound, suddenly, and he sits down on the kitchen chair as pins and needles creep up his legs and spine to be just as quickly replaced by the familiar, floating feeling of comfort. The kitchen clock skips from 10:00 to 10:17. Bren stretches and scratches his head, tracing shivers across his scalp. He feels nice, detached, like he could just drift right off to sleep. He stretches again, because it feels nice. He crosses his arms on the cold surface of the table and pillows his head on them.

Hello.

'Hi.'

Don't you like cake?

Bren smiles. The dreams you get, they're so vivid. He's always been good at telling himself stories.

'I liked cake.'

Why didn't you eat it then?

'I'd already eaten.'

Bread and butter isn't a meal.

'How do you know I ate that?'

I watched you.

'Who are you?'

I'm Carmen.

Bren raises his head, focusing and looking around the kitchenette. From here he can see into the front room which adjoins, and out through the window into the blank, grey morning. The couch looks particularly inviting, but he's too cosy to move and he lets his head start to loll again, thinking, *How must this look? What must she think?*

'Hi Carmen. I'm Bren. How did you get in here?'

I'm like a vampire. You have to invite me in.

'I didn't open the door, did I?'

No. You drank the vodka.

Bren lets out an exhale that starts as a laugh but gasps past his lips. A second later and he can't think why it was he found that funny. That thought, about the vodka. The thought he thought about the vodka letting somebody in. The thought he thought whilst he was talking to himself; conversing with his own mind.

'What do you mean, I drank the vodka?'

I was already in the flat. I've always been here. With you. Then I was in the vodka and you drank it. Now I'm inside you. That means that I can talk to you.

'What do you mean, inside me?' He should probably be feeling panic, but all Bren feels is peace and warmth. 'Who are you?'

I'm Carmen, says the voice patiently, as if explaining to a child why they need to take their medicine. *I used to live here in this building but then I died and at first I was sad but then I found out how to talk to people again.*

'You're a ghost?'

I'm a spirit.

'Vodka's a spirit.'

I don't have to use vodka. I can use cake as well.

'What's the best thing to use?'

The best way in is through your veins.

After that, every time, she'd be hiding in his hit. The works laid out neatly for him on the kitchen table: Bren never quite remembers putting them there but there they'd be, inviting as a door ajar.

He finds her pleasant company. Good conversation and silences which are never awkward. Comforting, somehow, like a part of him. Less intrusive than Lyndsey, which is weird considering some of the things that Carmen says.

I can see your insides.

'What do they look like?'

Pearly, Carmen says, *like pearls. Like the insides of shells and the creatures inside of shells, all washed with pink blood and pulsing fast as anemones.* Bren feels a queasy sort of lurch at that and she says, *I saw that; I saw your butterflies* and Bren feels, just for a moment, what it must be like to have somebody really understand you.

'How do you get out again?'

When Carmen is in, she doesn't stay in for long; just as long as the buzz stays, so Bren knows he'll always need one more try for elusive perfection.

Do you really want to know?

Bren laughs a falling-leaves laugh. 'You don't go in my wee do you?'

Sometimes. I pass through you; in your sweat or into the toilet. I'm in your tears and you breathe me out. There are traces of me lingering in your hair, knitted into your bones. Even if you leave I'll always be a part of you, a stitch in your fabric that you can't unpick without unravelling.

'That's nice.'

Is it?

'Yeah.'

That you can never escape me?

'That you'll never leave me.'

When Bren pees, he inspects it for clues. His piss in the bowl is tinged pink as icing. He thinks of Carmen, maybe swimming down there, a little cartoon ghost doing backstroke, and sometimes he doesn't flush. Or perhaps he just forgets to. Maybe that's how she always comes back. He pictures her as air, a glittering vapour, haloing him. He thinks of stories about guardian angels. Of insubstantial, momentous things like souls, or soulmates. He imagines breathing her in, in his sleep. He drifts into unconsciousness nightly, smiling at the darkness.

The thing that Bren likes best is when Carmen tells him stories of long ago when she was alive, when films were still black and white and the monochrome world outside was still in colour.

When I lived here this was all one house and not apartments. There were parties: the ladies wore mink and the gentlemen all drove Rolls-Royces. Everything was bright and crystal clear: we drank champagne from crystal flutes then, and there was a crystal chandelier in the ballroom. There was dancing until dawn on a sprung oak floor and the sun was always shining on the yellow sand. I wore pink and pearls and white silk gloves. I can't remember the colour of my eyes, but I know my favourite colour was pink. And there was always dancing.

Bren looks out of the window at the listless sea. He drags a knuckle through the condensation there, drawing the shape of a heart. One droplet detaches and runs the length of the pane, like a tear. He says,

'I'd like a Rolls-Royce.'

You have me instead, says Carmen.

One afternoon when Bren peels himself out of bed for another duel with the daytime, there is a tumbler of clear liquid and two tablets waiting for him on the kitchen table and it takes him a moment to remember that Lyndsey hasn't been round for nearly three months. He picks up the glass and sniffs it. It's tap water. The tablets, calciferous and white, about the size of a one penny coin; they appear to be aspirin. When he drops one into the glass of water, it rockets to the surface with an effervescent hiss. Bren frowns,

'Carmen? Where's my...?'

But of course, Carmen can't answer until Bren has swallowed the melted aspirin.

Take two a day with water, Carmen says.

'Why?'

It's good for you.

'I've never taken any before.'

Then it's a good time to start.

The day after that, Bren sets up his works himself, but then forgets to take his aspirin. It's hours later, when he's starting to feel the pinch of reality again that he realises that something was missing from his last hit. She hadn't been there, to lull him with fairy tales of the past whilst he dozed beneath the callous white face of the tutting kitchen clock, and he's assailed by how lonely he is, without Carmen. He feels absurd but compelled to apologise somehow, to tempt her back. He plumps the flat cushions on the couch and blows the dust off the lid of his record player, slotting in spitting vinyl to play yesterday's jazz. He even forces down a sandwich, but he's still alone. When upstairs starts to bang on the ceiling, he turns the music off and sits, gazing out of the window at the grey day, until he remembers, finally, the aspirin. When he's swallowed the bitter fizz of it, she says, *Don't forget again.*

'I won't forget. I missed you.'

If you keep on forgetting, you won't have the opportunity to miss me.

'What do you mean by that?'

Take two a day, with water.

'What do you mean by that?' Bren says, out loud, to his empty kitchen. 'Carmen, what have you seen in there?'

But nobody answers.

We're a long time dead; can we really blame our predecessors if they occasionally get a little restless, and give in to the temptation to make their presence known? Here's Alice Adams to show us the other side of a haunting.

Watching Kate & Gustav

Alice Adams

Even while I was still alive I was more naturally disposed to being an observer than a participant; my urge to action would wither in the face of an opportunity to fade quietly into the background and allow a story to unfold before me, unaffected by my presence. I'd once said as much to my husband and he'd told me that this was impossible. Quantum indeterminacy, Benedict – ever the physicist – had said: the very act of observation affects the outcome of the event you observe. Not long after I died, he left and I stayed here in the house. Without being told, I knew the rules, knew that I didn't have the option of leaving. The house was still and lonely without him. Little drifts of dust slowly accumulated in the hallways and corners. I would watch through the window as my neighbours went to and fro, occasionally stopping to exchange greetings and gossip in the square outside, but though I strained to hear them I could never quite make out their words.

After several months on my own it came as quite a relief when Kate and Gustav moved in. My new companions were a lively young couple and they filled the house with noise, Kate with her off-key singing and Gustav with his booming laugh that shook the furniture. They brought with them a large, gloomy tabby cat. In the evenings they liked to sit in the kitchen, drinking wine and talking about philosophy and politics, soap operas and celebrities. I adored sitting with them on those evenings, unseen and unheard, just watching.

I was worried at first that the cat might be able to see me. I sometimes fancied that he was following me with his eyes. Wherever I hovered, he seemed to gaze morosely in my direction. But in any case, he treated me with the same indifference as he treated his owners so after a time I stopped letting it concern me and we all settled down to a harmonious existence. Eventually, and I suppose inevitably, our peace was disturbed one morning by an insistent banging on the front door, heralding the arrival of Mrs Bennett from number four. Within minutes of being invited in for a cup of tea she had started to tell Kate about me.

'You're ever so brave,' she told her. 'I'm not sure I could live in a house where such a tragedy had occurred.'

'Tragedy?' Kate asked, 'What tragedy?' and of course the old busybody seized her chance.

'Oh, I'm terribly sorry, I didn't realise that Benedict hadn't told you when he let the place to you. His wife, it was, murdered by an intruder the police said. She died right here in this very room. Poor Benedict found her body. I just assumed you knew,' she said gleefully.

Kate turned rather pale and when Mrs Bennett had finally left, she walked back into the living room and seemed to look around carefully.

'Hello?' she called in a reedy voice, and although I didn't think it was possible for her to see me, I darted behind the bookcase just in case.

I'm not sure how I would have looked to her if she *could* have registered my presence; I imagine myself as appearing like a mote of dust in a ray of sunlight, a sort of twinkling point of singularity suspended in the air. At least, that had been my own first impression of myself once I had died. I had sat down intending to read, but my book had lain unopened in my lap and instead I was looking dreamily out of the window, watching the autumn day give way to dusk. My reverie must have been profound, for I didn't hear him move up behind me, and was entirely unaware of his presence until just a moment before I felt the first blow shudder through my head. The second and then the third blows arrived before I had time to turn or even to raise my hands, and I felt my essence being wrenched away from my body in fits and starts until all that remained of me was a speck of consciousness, an infinitely bright pinprick of light suspended against the velvet darkness of the universe.

I have no way of knowing how long the process lasted, but when I tuned back in to my surroundings little seemed to have changed. Or perhaps it had; I seemed to be viewing the world through a slightly distorted lens. I bobbed over to the window. The sky was turning silvery and the softening light was blurring the lines of the buildings on the opposite side of the square. Down in the street below, the traffic lights changed to green and a waiting car gunned its engine and moved forward. I looked back into the darkening room and registered my discarded body for the first time, torso slumped forward and sideways over the arm of the chair, one leg poking out from the bottom of my skirt at a strange angle, and the magnitude of what had happened sent me spinning across the room as if swept by a sudden gust of wind.

He was still standing behind the chair, still holding the wrench, but with his arms hanging limply at his sides now, and crying in a way that I had never seen him cry in all of our fifteen years of marriage, silently and barely moving, tears trickling from glazed eyes and running down ashen cheeks before dropping to the floor where they mingled with the slowly expanding pool of blood. I felt certain that I ought to be feeling betrayed and angry so I tried thinking to myself, how *could* he, how *dare* he; but perhaps death alters one's perspective on these things, because my outrage was at most half-hearted, and all that I really found myself feeling as I watched Benedict cry was terribly, dreadfully sad.

Kate seemed to become nervous after Mrs Bennett's visit, and I heard her tell Gustav that she wasn't sure she wanted to live in a house where someone had been killed. What if there was an unhappy spirit in the house, she asked him, and though he scoffed and laughed until she joined in, she still seemed anxious whenever she was alone.

I wondered how I could keep her from wanting to leave and reassure her that she had nothing to fear from me.

Then a few days later, while floating through the living room wall, I noticed a bundle of old photographs and letters down behind the bookcase, and on closer inspection realised that they were my own and must have fallen down there when we had still been living in the house. I had an idea: perhaps those letters, sent to me by friends in happier times, would show Kate what a gentle person I had been, not at all the type to come back as a malign presence.

With several hours' exertion, I managed to push them out from behind the bookcase just far enough, and she spotted them early that afternoon as she walked into the living room holding a mug of coffee. She picked up the bundle and carried it over to the armchair by the window, where she sat for at least an hour with her legs tucked beneath her, reading letter after letter and browsing through the photographs. I hovered nearby, watching for her reaction. Several times she returned to look at one photograph in particular, a picture that Benedict had taken of me many years earlier when I had been around Kate's own age, twenty-three or twenty-four. In the picture I was standing next to a tree, only half-smiling at the camera, a reluctant subject. I was wearing my hair in a long bob style just like Kate's, but dyed a glowing red in a rare act of rebellion.

I expected Kate to show the letters to Gustav that evening, but she didn't mention them. The next morning, once Gustav had left for work, she retrieved the bundle from her drawer and spent another hour gazing at the photographs and reading the letters. At around lunchtime, she put on her coat and left the house. She returned an hour later carrying a paper bag from the pharmacy and went straight into the bathroom. When she came out her hair was wet and at first I didn't realise what she had done, but as soon as she turned the hairdryer on I could see: she had dyed it bright red. She went into the living room and stood in front of the mirror above the fireplace, holding the photograph of me up next to her face and looking from one to the other and back again. I was rather shocked, but I couldn't help being just the smallest bit flattered.

'What on earth have you done to your hair?' exclaimed Gustav when he came home that evening.

'I just felt like a change,' she told him, giving him a twirl.

In the weeks that followed, I had the distinct impression that she knew I was there, but it no longer seemed to upset her. I didn't think she could see me, but she had noticed the cat glowering into empty air, and often followed its gaze to try to find its point of focus. Mrs Bennett was more than happy to elaborate on her story the next time she dropped round. She had always found me to be a lovely woman, just lovely. It had been terribly hard on poor Benedict. She, Mrs Bennett, had been round to clean the house and make him a hot dinner every day in the weeks following the tragedy, but he had soon realised that he could neither bear to live in the house any longer nor to sell it, and had decided to move out and find tenants.

On hearing the doorbell ring the following day I groaned inwardly, expecting it to be our neighbour again. When Kate opened the door she didn't recognise Benedict, having met him briefly only once, and I almost didn't recognise him myself, his face was so distorted by shock.

'Hello?' Kate prompted him, but although he managed to close his mouth he was still too disturbed to assemble a sentence. As he forced his face into a more normal expression, Kate finally recognised him, and realised the cause of his reaction.

'You're Benedict, aren't you? Come in,' she told him softly.

He followed her along the corridor and into the kitchen, unable to take his eyes off her.

'I was just passing,' he finally said. 'I thought I might stop by to see if there was any post for me.'

Tearing his gaze from her, he turned away, belatedly trying to conceal the extent of his distress. Kate reached out towards him, put her hand on his arm.

'It's the hair, isn't it?' she said. 'You thought I was her.'

As he turned and raised his head I caught a glimpse of the man I had loved for almost half a lifetime. He had aged enormously in the months since I had died, the infinite familiarity of his features marked by the alien lines of grief and remorse etched across them, his eyes pulsing with near-luminous torment. I was overwhelmed by the need to comfort him. As he raised his gaze to meet Kate's, I flew up and settled myself onto the surface of her left eye, where I sat twinkling and glowing until Benedict's eyes locked onto hers. He leant closer and touched his lips to hers and we stood together, the three of us, for an endless moment in which the lips against his were mine, and the hand on his arm belonged to me so much that I could feel the rough fabric of his shirt against my fingers.

And then as quickly as it arrived, the moment was over and Kate and Benedict sprang back from one another in a flurry of apologies, *Sorry, sorry I don't know what came over me, why I.... No, I'm sorry, I can't imagine what you must be feeling, I shouldn't be confusing you like this...* and he was gone, and she was left standing alone in the kitchen, holding her fingertips up to her lips.

A few days later it was Gustav who took the telephone call while Kate and I listened grimly, understanding easily from his side of the conversation that Benedict was selling the house and they could no longer stay there. Two short weeks later they were gone and I was alone with the drifting dust in the silent house again, cursing myself for my interference, my failure to have understood that I must only watch, and not intervene in the affairs of the living. I spend the days now trailing from room to room, missing Kate's ecstatic chatter and Gustav's avalanches of laughter, even missing the attentions of the gloomy cat. I won't make the same mistakes with the next people, I promise myself. Next time I will only watch.

Jane Alexander took first prize in the 2014 Fiction Desk Ghost Story Competition for this poignant and original spin on the traditional Scottish ballad Tam Lin. *We've reprinted the ballad itself in full after the story.*

In Yon Green Hill to Dwell

Jane Alexander

O I forbid you, maidens a',
That wear gowd on your hair,
To come or gae by Carterhaugh,
For young Tam Lin is there.

'Forbidden,' I say. 'That had something to do with it.' The word sounds like an invitation. That lift in its middle, flicking up: like raised eyebrows, or the hook of a glance. I say it again, for the hard-and-soft sound of it, for the way it contains its opposite. 'When you're that age – what was I? Sixteen –'

'Seventeen,' says Tam. It's the first he's said, all session. As if it matters.

'My dad should've known,' I say. 'I mean. I was off the rails anyway.' I can feel my mouth tugging into a smile: I was wild, once.

'Tam?' says the counsellor. 'What about you? Was it significant for you, that Janet's father disapproved?'

'Ach,' he says, and though I'm not looking at him, I know he's shaking his head. I can *hear* it. 'No. Maybe. I don't know.'

What a way he has with words: my silver-tongued poet.

He was the prize, back then. He'd turn up every now and then, in the woods by the well where we used to hang out: tight black jeans and a military coat, silver hipflask wedged in his pocket. He was older than the rest of us. When he said he was a poet, we laughed, but despite ourselves we were impressed. I'd never thought of a poet as someone alive, let alone blue-eyed and beautiful.

While the rest of the lassies fluttered about him, hitching up skirts and tugging down necklines, I acted like he wasn't there. Like he wasn't in my dreams at night, golden, glowing; like I didn't wake feverish at dawn, clutching a sweat-damp pillow. I was hooked on the high of his eyes on me, his watchful half-smiles, the way he saw straight through me. It was a game, addictive, and we kept on playing till the day I skived school to turn up alone. Till the day it was just us two.

It happens occasionally, in this bland pastel room: a moment when it's us two alone. When the counsellor's listening to the words, but deaf to their significance.

'Change,' he says now, 'can be positive in a relationship. But it can be hard, as well.' He nods his head, agreeing with himself.

'Well,' I say, 'we've certainly had our share of change.' I glance at Tam, who's avoiding my gaze, looking off into the corner; see the muscles shift under his skin. Not a smile, but at least the suggestion of one. The counsellor keeps on nodding. I notice him noticing, catching at our hidden current of meaning. How his face slips – the open face he wears as a mask – and how he hides the slip with an all-purpose smile. It makes me want to stir things up.

'It was *her* that did it,' I say. 'It was her that changed him.'

'When you say *her*, you're talking about the woman Tam was seeing –'

'I'd hardly call her a woman!'

The counsellor's face slips even further. He thinks I'm reduced by burning jealousy to insults and insinuations. But there's an upward twitch at the corner of Tam's lips, and for a moment – just a moment – it's me and him together.

The things that bind you: shared traumas, shared secrets. I thought we'd be bound right till the end. Tighter than promises, tighter than rings.

'She wasn't a woman,' I say. 'She was impossible.'

In the woods by the well, just us two. When he tipped his head to swig from that silver flask, the curve of his white throat begged to be touched. He told me I was special, precious, I was The One. I raised his flask to my lips, a burning kiss: spiced, bright, nothing I had a name for. I'd worked my way through the boys my age, so plain and tame and tongue-tied. I was ready for something wilder. Minutes later, his hand up my skirt, my hands unsnaking his belt. No-one for miles around: still, I felt watched.

After, curled into each other, bedded in ivy; that's when he told me. Said he belonged to someone else. *Save me*, he said. His face was naked, his blue eyes haunted. *Save me.* I thought he meant he was married – my wife doesn't understand me – but when I laughed, he started to shake. Drugs, I thought then, a proper habit, and scanned his arms for trackmarks. But he was smooth skinned, life strong in his veins.

No wonder she took a fancy to him; claimed him for her own.

What made me believe him, in the end? His impossible story? Why didn't I think he was mad, or tripping? His silver tongue, it must have been. I lay in his arms, and promised him. I lay in his arms: inside of me, everything changing. A magic spell. A spell of division, of doubling and doubling.

The counsellor reckons we've got issues with trust. Well. Tam might have told me first, before he knocked me up.

All the last hour I've done the talking while Tam's sat there like a pudding: single words dragged out of him, given up like gold coins. Now, in the car, I keep my mouth shut. I don't start the engine, or turn on the radio. Dusk presses against the windscreen. A line of trees, newly stripped, shivers its branches in the wind. A small witch clings to her hat as she skips down the street; behind her a skeleton, not much taller, shields the guttering flame of his turnip lantern. I sit – wait – swallow the starts of a dozen sentences, till finally Tam caves in, and cracks the stubborn silence.

'We'll need to be heading back,' he says.

A skirl of leaves blows past the window. Six words: it's a start. 'Used to be,' I say, 'I couldn't shut you up.'

'Two hours, I said to Ann-Marie. She'll be wanting to get away.'

'Not that I wanted to shut you up. But now...'

'Janet, come on –'

'No!' I bang the heel of my hand against the steering wheel. 'No: you come on. What are we doing? What's the point of this? Are we giving up, is that it? Because I don't give up, I hang on, that's what I do – of all people, you know that. But what am I hanging on to?'

For a minute, I'm sure I've talked him back into silence. Then: 'All that,' he says. 'In there. What you were saying, how she was impossible.' I nod, not wanting to open my mouth in case it gives him an excuse to shut his. 'And so she was,' he says. 'But what you want ... that's more impossible still.' He looks at me. 'Well, unless you've got a time machine? To turn us back, that's what you want. Back seven years.'

I'm ready to argue, but he raises a hand like a wall between us.

'Listen,' he says. He sounds tired. Defeated. 'I'm yours. Yours and Caitlin's. I stay home, keep it nice, look after my daughter. That's all I need, and there's not many men would do that. But that's not enough for you. It's not how you want me. You want me on loan.'

He looks at me like he's asked me a question, but the arguments have died on my lips.

'You want me bewitched by her, still.'

And pleasant is the fairy land,
But, an eerie tale to tell,
Ay at the end of seven years
We pay a tiend to hell;
I am sae fair and fu o flesh,
I'm feard it be mysel.

There's a flash of it when he thanks the babysitter, after I've paid her. The lassie from over the road: almost the age I was when we met. He turns it on just a wee bit, the old warmth, the spark, holding her eyes a second too long – and I should be smashing plates, shouldn't I, yelling that he never looks at me that way. But I don't. I shove the fish fingers under the grill and slop the baked beans into the pan and tell Caitlin ten minutes until tea.

'Look,' says Caitlin, 'we made hats!'

I'm wrestling with the gas which is all sorts of temperamental and thinking how we can't afford a new hob and wondering whether Tam can fix it, and she's dancing about waiting for me to admire, singing about witches and black cats. Eventually I get the gas to stay lit, and turn to look at my daughter. She's sporting a black paper hat, wonky brimmed and crusted with glitter stars, accessorised with a pair of pink gauze wings.

'I'm a witch,' she tells me, hand on hips.

'A witch, are you? Or a fairy?'

'I'm a princess-witch.'

I can't tell her to take it off. I can't tell her there's no such thing. I look to Tam for help.

'You look magic,' he says, manfully, and she does a spin, waves a wand made out of drinking straws.

The two of them head out after tea: he's promised to take her guising. I open a bottle of cheap wine, close my eyes as I drink. I imagine the glass is a hip flask, heavy silver, its threaded neck teasing the tip of my tongue; the alcohol heady with unnamed spices. In reality, it's sharp and watery. I swallow it down like medicine, pour some more.

Just once, he spoke to me. It was not long afterwards: we were at the start of our happy ending, and I still believed that, since it hadn't killed us, the trauma we'd shared made us indestructible. But if ever I spoke about what had happened, he changed the subject. Turned on the TV. Left the room.

That night, I was up feeding Caitlin, in the chair by the bedroom window; Tam muttering, twisting in his sleep, covers kicked onto the floor.

'What was it like?' I said, softly. 'Tam. I wish you'd speak to me. I wish you'd tell me.'

He opened his eyes, stared straight at me. I clutched at Caitlin, holding her closer.

'I was there,' he said. His voice was flat. 'I wasn't absent. I was the snake. I was the deer. I was the red-hot iron, and the ember.

She pulled me apart, re-made me. She destroyed me, again, again, again. Bones jagging into hooves. Tearing the skin. Poison still singing in the needles of my teeth. A rope of cold flesh – a tongue split in two – a scream of white heat –'

His face was pale, shined with sweat, his eyes unseeing. He looked like a dead man conjured back into life.

'But then,' I said, 'I saved you.' I stretched a hand towards him: to comfort? To plead? 'Remember, Tam? I saved you?'

In the morning, he'd forgotten he'd ever spoken.

The bottle's half gone by the time they get back. Caitlin's high on sweets and attention – she's been performing her party piece for the neighbours, her Halloween song about the witch's cat. She gives one last rendition: each time I think it's finished, there's another verse to come. When I'm certain she's done, I give her a round of applause and offer a bedtime story.

'No,' she says. 'I want Daddy to read it.' Nine times out of ten it's Daddy she wants.

'Okay, sleep tight, love you,' I say, and I sit back on the sagging couch and cradle my glass.

Sometimes, I think that's what spoiled us – my saving him. He begged me to do it: *hold me fast, don't let me pass.* But being saved is so passive. I won't read those stories to Caitlin about princesses waiting to be rescued, though god knows what Tam lets her do when I'm out earning our living. God knows what stories he's telling her now.

More often than not he'll fall asleep up there, stretched alongside her, feet hanging off the edge of the bed. When that happens, I don't wake him. But tonight, we're meant to be talking. Homework, the counsellor called it, as though we're studying for an exam, as though our performance will be assessed and graded: pass or fail. Tonight's exam topic is *expectations*; our objective, to find some middle ground. So I wait a while, long enough to finish the wine, then I haul myself up off the sofa and climb the stairs.

In Caitlin's room the nightlight is on, spinning stars around the ceiling. She's face down, breathing loud and deep, dead to the world. Beside her, Tam lies tense, chest barely lifting. I know he is faking.

I say his name, and his eyelids flicker.

'Homework,' I say. 'Expectations.'

A heavier breath: a sigh.

I speak softly, so as not to wake Caitlin. 'Are you thinking of her?'

He doesn't respond.

'Seven years with her. How could you not?' I'm making it easy for him to confess. I wish he'd tell me *yes*, tell me he thinks of her, often, always... 'Not even at night?' I say. 'Not even in your dreams?' In dreams: that's where I hear her. Cursing me like she did that night, ice and grit – and softer, more insidious: *got what you wanted, did you? Enjoying your fine husband? Your ill-gotten gains?*

He keeps his eyes shut, but he answers at last. 'If she's ever inside me,' he says, 'it's in my nightmares.'

I should walk away now, close the door, let him sleep. 'But you must... when you think of yourself back then... don't you ever want –'

'Let me tell you what I want,' he says. His voice is low and clear. 'I want to stay here, safe inside, in our house. I want to look after our daughter. I want to be here for her, always, so she never has to be afraid. This, here. This is what I want.'

A poet. What did it ever mean? A box of pamphlets I paid to have printed, taking up space, turning yellow. He couldn't give them away. The rhymes he makes for Caitlin, when there's plenty already in books.

I shouldn't drive – I've drunk too much – but I drain a glass of water, then another; grab my keys anyway. If I'm to make it to Milecross by midnight, there's no choice.

I duck through the rain and into the car. Rub my eyes to focus my vision. I set off carefully, watching out for late night guisers and Halloween revellers. For each beat of the windscreen wipers, I count three, four of my heart. The roads are empty, till my headlights illuminate a dark figure crossing ahead of me: a black cat raised up on two legs. She stops, stares at me. Then she laughs, turns tail and vanishes into the dark.

Just at the mirk and midnight hour
The fairy folk will ride,
And they that wad their true-love win,
At Miles Cross they maun bide.

I park across from the Co-op. As I hurry the short distance to the crossroads the church bells ring: once, twice, three times. Fifteen minutes to wait.

Here's where it happened, seven years ago: here, where a crumpled can of Special Brew catches the streetlights, and fag-ends lie scattered across the cobbles. Here's where I held him, held him fast, as he turned and turned in my arms. A red-hot iron burning clean through the skin of my hands. At least I knew I was alive; could feel it in that screaming pain, could smell it in my own roasting flesh.

And after – he couldn't stand. That's when I was most terrified. The shock of his skin, suddenly, and his whole weight on me as he fell to the frozen ground, fitting – kicking and shuddering. I laid my coat over him, put his head on my lap. Rubbed his shoulders, his arms, his body, trying to warm him. All the heat had gone from him, in the red-hot iron, in the burning coal. Everything that had been fire had turned to ice. And she, the Faerie Queen, was nowhere.

I wrap my arms around myself, pull my hood lower. You want me bewitched, he'd said. Bewitched by her still. And I wonder was it always true, from the first time I saw him; that the glow of him, the gold that drew me, was only the glitter of some other woman's treasure?

It starts with the first chime of midnight: a faint rumble that could be thunder – except that the rain has faded to a smirr; except that it keeps on rolling, building, turning into the drum of unshod hooves on cobblestones. I stare, straining into the street-lit dark. I can't see the riders, though they must be close now. I take a step forward, placing myself in their path. In the dark, a deeper shadow, spreading, growing; the hairs on my arms stand up. I can feel the wind of them, the air shifting – the hoofbeats loud now, deafening – and I close my eyes and raise my arms and pray she'll see me: *stop, stop* –

A sudden stillness. Small sounds all around me. The creak of leather. The shuffle of hooves. Close enough to touch. I open my eyes. Look up.

The horse towers over me, flesh and blood, white and groomed and glossy, all muscle and sinew under its shining coat. Breath plumes from its flaring nostrils – but there's no heat. If I reached to touch, my leather-sheathed fingers would freeze and crack. And if I touched my fingertips to a riding boot, a stockinged knee, or a hiked-up skirt; what then? Above me she sits as on a throne, her face in shadow.

'Bold Janet,' she says, and I can hear amusement in her voice, which is icicles on the nape of my neck, is the voice I've dreamed for seven years. She laughs. 'Bold, or boneheaded.'

I feel it then: the army of riders massed at her back. Not that she needs an army. I've seen what she can do on a whim.

'Or both,' I say. 'Why not?'

'Careful, Janet. Is that your question?'

'My question?'

She breathes an Arctic sigh. 'You've something to ask. Of course you have. Married him, didn't you; had his daughter. But here you are alone. Well, ask carefully. I'll answer just the once.'

Perhaps there's a break in the clouds; perhaps up there the moon is full, because for a moment I see her clearly. Her lips are curved, her eyes slanted: cruel, beautiful. She knows. She knows what I've come to ask.

Change him back. Take him back. Change him, one more time.

But I hear his voice. I remember his words. *What you want is impossible.* I see them together, him and Caitlin. *This, here. This is what I want.* Curled around each other, sleeping safe. *To never be afraid.*

At the edge of my hearing, a siren rises and falls, its urgency faded by distance; like a reminder of something, like the loosest stitch still tacking me to this town, this life, this world. Then a horse shifts its hooves – sharp, soft, soft: a single bar of a waltz – and its harness shakes, sings, strikes a golden note that hangs in front of me. Close enough, bright enough, almost, to touch.

The smirr has coated me, given me an ice-damp skin. When I press my lips together I taste it: when I open them, I'm ready to ask.

'Take me?' I say. 'Take me.'

The inspiration behind Jane Alexander's 'In Yon Green Hill to Dwell', Tam Lin appears here in full. Various versions of this traditional Scottish ballad exist, with the earliest known reference to the story dating back to 1549. The following version was recorded by Robert Burns, and appears in Francis James Child's 1884 book The English and Scottish Popular Ballads.

Tam Lin

Traditional

O I forbid you, maidens a',
  That wear gowd on your hair,
To come or gae by Carterhaugh,
  For young Tam Lin is there.

There's nane that gaes by Carterhaugh
  But they leave him a wad,
Either their rings, or green mantles,
  Or else their maidenhead.

Janet has kilted her green kirtle
  A little aboon her knee,
And she has broded her yellow hair
  A little aboon her bree,
And she's awa to Carterhaugh
  As fast as she can hie.

When she came to carterhaugh
  Tam Lin was at the well,
And there she fand his steed standing,
  But away was himsel.

She had na pu'd a double rose,
  A rose but only twa,
Till upon then started young Tam Lin,
  Says, Lady, thou's pu nae mae.

Why pu's thou the rose, Janet,
  And why breaks thou the wand?
Or why comes thou to Carterhaugh
  Withoutten my command?

'Carterhaugh, it is my own,
  My daddy gave it me,
I'll come and gang by Carterhaugh,
  And ask nae leave at thee.'

Janet has kilted her green kirtle
  A little aboon her knee,
And she has snooded her yellow hair
  A little aboon her bree,
And she is to her father's ha,
  As fast as she can hie.

Four and twenty ladies fair
  Were playing at the ba,
And out then came the fair Janet,
  The flower among them a'.

Four and twenty ladies fair
  Were playing at the chess,
And out then came the fair Janet,
  As green as onie glass.

Out then spake an auld grey knight,
  Lay oer the castle wa,
And says, Alas, fair Janet, for thee,
  But we'll be blamed a'.

'Haud your tongue, ye auld fac'd knight,
  Some ill death may ye die!
Father my bairn on whom I will,
  I'll father none on thee.'

Out then spak her father dear,
  And he spak meek and mild,
'And ever alas, sweet Janet,' he says,
  'I think thou gaest wi child.'

'If that I gae wi child, father,
  Mysel maun bear the blame,
There's neer a laird about your ha,
  Shall get the bairn's name.

'If my love were an earthly knight,
  As he's an elfin grey,
I wad na gie my ain true-love
  For nae lord that ye hae.

'The steed that my true love rides on
  Is lighter than the wind,
Wi siller he is shod before,
  Wi burning gowd behind.'

Janet has kilted her green kirtle
  A little aboon her knee,
And she has snooded her yellow hair
  A little aboon her bree,
And she's awa to Carterhaugh
  As fast as she can hie.

When she came to Carterhaugh,
  Tam Lin was at the well,
And there she fand his steed standing,
  But away was himsel.

She had na pu'd a double rose,
  A rose but only twa,
Till up then started young Tam Lin,
  Says, Lady, thou pu's nae mae.

'Why pu's thou the rose, Janet,
  Amang the groves sae green,
And a' to kill the bonny babe
  That we gat us between?'

'O tell me, tell me, Tam Lin,' she says,
  'For's sake that died on tree,
If eer ye was in holy chapel,
  Or christendom did see?'

'Roxbrugh he was my grandfather,
  Took me with him to bide
And ance it fell upon a day
  That wae did me betide.

'And ance it fell upon a day
  A cauld day and a snell,
When we were frae the hunting come,
  That frae my horse I fell,
The Queen o' Fairies she caught me,
  In yon green hill do dwell.

'And pleasant is the fairy land,
  But, an eerie tale to tell,
Ay at the end of seven years,
  We pay a tiend to hell,
I am sae fair and fu o flesh,
  I'm feard it be mysel.

'But the night is Halloween, lady,
  The morn is Hallowday,
Then win me, win me, an ye will,
  For weel I wat ye may.

'Just at the mirk and midnight hour
  The fairy folk will ride,
And they that wad their true-love win,
  At Miles Cross they maun bide.'

'But how shall I thee ken, Tam Lin,
  Or how my true-love know,
Amang sa mony unco knights,
  The like I never saw?'

'O first let pass the black, lady,
  And syne let pass the brown,
But quickly run to the milk-white steed,
  Pu ye his rider down.

'For I'll ride on the milk-white steed,
  And ay nearest the town,
Because I was an earthly knight
  They gie me that renown.

'My right hand will be gloved, lady,
  My left hand will be bare,
Cockt up shall my bonnet be,
  And kaimed down shall my hair,
And thae's the takens I gie thee,
  Nae doubt I will be there.

'They'll turn me in your arms, lady,
  Into an esk and adder,
But hold me fast, and fear me not,
  I am your bairn's father.

'They'll turn me to a bear sae grim,
  And then a lion bold,
But hold me fast, and fear me not,
  And ye shall love your child.

'Again they'll turn me in your arms
  To a red het gand of airn,
But hold me fast, and fear me not,
  I'll do you nae harm.

'And last they'll turn me in your arms
  Into the burning gleed,
Then throw me into well water,
  O throw me in with speed.

'And then I'll be your ain true-love,
  I'll turn a naked knight,
Then cover me wi your green mantle,
  And hide me out o sight.'

Gloomy, gloomy was the night,
  And eerie was the way,
As fair Jenny in her green mantle
  To Miles Cross she did gae.

At the mirk and midnight hour
  She heard the bridles sing,
She was as glad at that
  As any earthly thing.

First she let the black pass by,
  And syne she let the brown,
But quickly she ran to the milk-white steed,
  And pu'd the rider down.

Sae weel she minded what he did say,
  And young Tam Lin did win,
Syne covered him wi her green mantle,
  As blythe's a bird in spring

Out then spak the Queen o Fairies,
  Out of a bush o broom,
'Them that has gotten young Tam Lin
  Has gotten a stately groom.'

Out then spak the Queen o Fairies,
  And an angry woman was she,
'Shame betide her ill-far'd face,
  And an ill death may she die,
For she's taen awa the bonniest knight
  In a' my companie.

'But had I kend, Tam Lin,' said she,
  'What now this night I see,
I wad hae taen out thy twa grey een,
  And put in twa een o tree.'

About the Contributors

Alice Adams has had short stories published in *The Times* and various magazines, and is the author of two novels, one of which was shortlisted in the *Mslexia* unpublished novel competition and is about to be submitted to publishers by her literary agent.

She's done everything from waitressing to working in the City and her subject matter ranges across politics, economics, sex, drugs, poetry, maths, physics, philosophy, and the existence of God. She lives in North London but escapes into the wilderness as often as possible. Alice is currently working on her third novel and blogs on her Facebook page.

Jane Alexander lives in Edinburgh, and is currently working on a collection of uncanny short stories. Her first novel *The Last Treasure Hunt* will be published in 2015.

Die Booth lives in Chester and enjoys tea, cake, and exploring dark places. Die's short stories have featured in publications by Black & BLUE, *Litro*, Prime, and The Cheshire Prize for Literature. You can read more of Die's writing in debut novel *Spirit Houses*, and in *365 Lies* – a single author collection of one flash fiction for every day of the year, out now in support of the MNDA.

Lucinda Bromfield writes short stories and poetry. Her stories have been published in *Andromeda Spaceways Inflight Magazine* and *Ashton Walks*, a collection of short stories based in Bristol where she now lives. If she isn't writing, you'll find her gardening, cooking, hiking, or cleaning things.

Bernie Deehan's short stories have been published in *Vintage Script*, *Litro*, and other journals and websites, and some have been performed by actors at Liars' League events. You can read a few stories, and his blog, at berniedeehan.com and he's also on Twitter at @BernieDeehan

Tamsin Hopkins is making her first Fiction Desk appearance in this volume. She has a short story collection in the pipeline with Cinnamon Press, and you can find her on Twitter where she posts as @TamsinHopkins.

Matthew Licht is the author of the detective trilogy *World without Cops*, and several other novels. His two short story collections with Salt, *The Moose Show* and *Justine, Joe & The Zen Garbageman*, have been nominated for the Frank O'Connor Prize. He's obsessed with bicycles. Due to this, or as a consequence, he lives in Italy. 'Got to burn off the spaghetti somehow.'

Matthew's story 'Dave Tough's Luck' appeared in *Various Authors*, the first Fiction Desk anthology. 'Across the Kinderhook' appeared in *Crying Just Like Anybody*, and 'Washout' appeared in *New Ghost Stories.*

Amanda Mason is a graduate of Dartington College of Arts, where she studied theatre and began writing by devising and directing her own plays. After a few years of earning a very irregular living in lots of odd jobs, including performing in a comedy street magic act, she became a teacher and has worked in the UK, Italy, Spain, and Germany.

She now lives in York and writes plays, flash fiction, and short stories. Her work has been published in Cracked Eye's *Storms, Lies and Wildcards*, National Flash Fiction Day's 2014 anthology *Eating My Words*, and in Parthian Books' *A Flock of Shadows*. Her story 'No Good Deed' was included in The Fiction Desk's sixth anthology, *New Ghost Stories*.

Miha Mazzini is a Slovenian author, with 27 published books, translated into nine languages. His work has often been anthologised, including in the 2011 Pushcart prize anthology. He's also a screenwriter and director, and voting member of the European Film Academy. He has a PhD in Anthropology of Everyday Life.

Matt Plass lives in Sussex. He works in e-learning, previously edited *Tall Tales & Modern Fables* magazine and is one half of Bread and Love Productions.

'Next to Godliness' is Matt's fourth Fiction Desk story.

Melanie Whipman is a PhD student and an associate lecturer at the University of Chichester. Her MA in Creative Writing was awarded the Kate Betts Prize, and her work has been broadcast on Radio 4 and published in various anthologies and magazines. She is currently editing her short story collection, which will be published by Ink Tears in 2015.

For more information on the contributors
to this volume, please visit our website:

www.thefictiondesk.com/authors

Also Available

the first seven Fiction Desk anthologies:

1. Various Authors
2. All These Little Worlds
3. The Maginot Line
4. Crying Just Like Anybody
5. Because of What Happened
6. New Ghost Stories
7. There Was Once a Place

Subscribe

three volumes
for just £22
(in the UK, or £29 worldwide).

Subscribing to our anthology series is the best way to keep yourself supplied with the best new short fiction from the UK and abroad. It costs just £22 for three volumes within the UK, or £29 for a worldwide subscription.

(Prices correct at time of going to press, but may change over time; please see website for current pricing.)

---

www.thefictiondesk.com